CHERRINGHAM

A COSY MYSTERY SERIES

PLAYING DEAD

Neil Richards • Matthew Costello

RED DOG
UK

Cherringham is a long-running mystery series set in the Cotswolds. The stories are self-contained, though many will enjoy reading them in order of publication:

1.

ALL THE WORLD'S A STAGE

GETTING INTO THE deserted theatre had been easy. The alleyway at the back couldn't be seen from the High Street and the rubbish bins made for an easy step-up. The new dressing room windows hadn't shut properly since they'd been installed.

All he needed was a screwdriver to flip the catch and — *click* — the window opened easily.

He eased his legs over the window-sill and jumped down.

He was in.

He stood perfectly still in the darkness, not breathing, just listening to the old building.

Nothing.

He was alone.

He took out his pencil torch, flicked it on and checked his watch: 10 p.m. Rehearsals had finished at nine. Nobody would be coming back into the building at this hour. By now they were all in the Angel across the road, well into their second pints.

As long as he didn't make a noise, he could do what he had to do and be home by ten thirty. Maybe he'd even have time to pop innocently into the pub for a swift half himself...

He slipped out of the dressing room into the corridor. Somehow at night, the smell of new paint in here seemed stronger.

He hardly needed the torch. Even with the recent renovations, he knew the layout of the rooms and corridors so well. Two fire doors — then the set of stairs — and now, here he was.

In the auditorium, just below the apron.

He flicked the torch around the space. Pristine rows of new seats, sloping up to the rear of the theatre until they were lost under the balcony. High windows at the sides, letting in a faint orange glow from the street lights outside.

He could see the fire exit signs glowing softly green. And up above, the Victorian stucco work; spotless. Cherubs playing harps, the gods of theatre drinking wine and looking jovially down.

Wasn't like this when I was a kid.

He thought back to all those Saturday mornings sitting in here with his other Cherringham mates, watching films on the rickety old screen, throwing popcorn around, shouting, mucking about.

Watching the older kids snogging in the back row.

God, it stank then. But now, with all that Lottery money thrown at it, the whole place ripped out and refurbished — the Cherringham Little Theatre was a building to be proud of.

Rebuilt inside and out with all the latest digital sound equipment and lights. A full schedule of music, comedy and theatre lined up well into next Spring.

And of course the Players, Cherringham's very own amateur dramatic company, in residence with three productions planned for the inaugural year.

Shame the pompous idiots who ran the company couldn't

make better decisions. Couldn't judge people.

Didn't understand *feelings*.

His anger welled up again, but he calmed himself, took a deep breath.

No need to be angry. He was going to fix things, wasn't he? That's why he was here.

He climbed the three steps on to the stage and slipped through the black drapes into the wings. Back here, he really did need the torch. Not a chink in the curtains for any light to get in.

He shone his torch up into the rigging above the stage.

He could see the thick metal bar which ran stage left to stage right. Various lanterns and spotlights hung down from it. Chains and ropes curled away from the bar towards the back of the stage, behind the scenery.

He knew from experience how heavy the lanterns and spots were. It was a two-man job setting up the lighting rig and safety was a constant mantra.

You didn't want a light slipping from up there and dropping on to the stage. Especially during a performance. Crowded stage, actors below, concentrating on performance, listening for cues. Last thing they'd do would be to think of looking up — even if they heard a noise.

Five kilos — maybe ten — of sharp-edged metal, falling twenty feet.

That would hurt.

No. Would do more than hurt.

Could *kill*.

On a whim, he stepped out on to the stage again and sank down on one knee, facing the invisible audience.

"If it were done when 'tis done, then 'twere well it were done quickly," he said, his voice seeming to fill the theatre.

He couldn't remember the rest of the speech.

He got up and checked that he still had the spanner nestled in his pocket. Then he headed over to the steel ladder on the side wall, put the torch in his mouth and started to climb up into the lighting rig...

I would have killed in that part, he thought.

2.

ON YOUR MARKS

GRAHAM JONES STOOD in the wings and felt another bead of cold sweat roll down his back. He stared at the rehearsal script clenched in his hands and tried to memorise the speech, but the words just seemed to *swim* in front of his eyes.

He looked at the other cast members on the stage in front of him. All merrily acting away — without their scripts!

What was wrong with him? Why couldn't he do this? Why was he the only one still — what did they call it? — on script?

All this jargon. Marks. Calls. *Flies.*

It was all a terrible, terrible mistake.

He wasn't an *actor*. He'd never done it before. What could possibly have made him think that he would be able to do this?

Greed? Pride? No. Love, plain and simple.

Ellie, barmaid down at the Ploughman's had signed up for the auditions months back when the new theatre was announced and the Players issued their call for new talent. And she'd got the part as the leading lady!

Beautiful Ellie who pulled the pints and always gave him a special smile.

That smile, it's got to mean something — hasn't it? he thought.

He never had the courage to really talk to her there — the

place was always so full of other men — well, it would be wouldn't it? It was a pub after all.

But here, these regular evening rehearsals, surely here if he got a small part too, then she'd chat with him, and get to know him and then like him, and maybe even fall in love with him…

His mind always raced ahead with the fantasy.

And then they'd get married and she'd move in with him and his son and they'd all live happily ever after.

So he'd gone to the auditions and amazingly he *had* got the part and now—

"Hello, Graham! Earth calling Graham!" came the shrill voice of the director, Jez Kramer, from the stage.

Graham looked up and to his horror saw Kramer and the rest of the cast on stage, frozen, arms folded, all staring at him.

"For God's sake Graham, are you *ever* going to hear your cue?"

"Oh — gosh — sorry, I—"

"Don't give me apologies, per-lease. Just give me your Police Constable Bull before we all die of shame out here!"

"Oh, right. Yes…"

Graham took a deep breath, marched on to the stage and looked for his mark, as he'd been taught.

Phew, there it is, he thought, spotting the small chalk circle on the wooden stage floor right next to Jez.

He positioned himself on it, then turned to face the auditorium.

"Well then, well then," he said in his best police-acting-voice. "I hear there's been a crime committed."

"There certainly has, ladies and gentlemen," said Jez, pointing straight at him. "This man has been caught impersonating an actor!"

For a second, Graham thought he must have got the page

wrong. He didn't recognise that line. But then he saw the cast burst out laughing. And he even heard snickering and laughter from backstage too.

They were all laughing at him.

This is so unfair, he thought. But then he laughed too.

Jez Kramer was a bully. And Graham knew how to deal with bullies. He'd dealt with them all his life. His solution was to surrender completely to them, to laugh at himself louder than they did and just put up with the humiliation.

Because eventually bullies got bored and they picked a new victim.

At least that was the idea.

He watched as Jez stepped closer and put an arm around his shoulder. Graham was familiar with this gesture. To the others it would look like friendly reconciliation. But he knew it was really subjugation. Manipulation.

"Graham, Graham, Graham," said Jez in a chummy voice. "Whatever are we going to do with you?"

"I don't know, Jez," said Graham.

"Maybe we should stick you on a rocket and fire you on to the stage?"

"That would be funny," said Graham. "But then you'd probably have to fire me off again."

He watched Jez laugh. But he could also see that Jez was scrutinising him, making sure that Graham wasn't taking the piss.

"Very good, Graham," he said. "Just one teeny, teeny note though: do remember to address your line to the actors — not the audience."

"Yes, yes. Of course."

"You're the local bobby, Graham. Called to the country residence of Lord and Lady Blake here…"

Jez gestured to the other two actors, Helen Edwards and Ambrose Goode. Graham nodded to them and felt reassured when he saw them smile back. Helen and Ambrose were old-school. Not newcomers, like Jez.

He realised Jez was still speaking and tried to concentrate again:

"…to investigate a priceless pearl which has gone missing."

"Yes, yes, sorry Jez."

"And do remember — it's a serious whodunit, darling — not a Ray Cooney farce."

He watched Jez step back. He seemed to be satisfied that Graham had got the point.

"Tell you what, Jez," said Ambrose. "Why not get him to come in stage left instead? That way you can just give him the nod if he misses your cue."

Graham watched Jez consider the actor's suggestion.

"Splendid idea, Ambrose!" he said. "Brilliant, in fact. Perhaps *you* should be directing this."

Graham felt the air on stage grow even colder.

"Well, I was, wasn't I," said Ambrose sullenly. "Until you—"

"Stage left, it is then," said Jez, ignoring him.

"Stage left?" said Graham.

"Yes, Graham," he said, pointing to the wings. "The opposite of stage *right*. God. Just over there."

Graham nodded. It seemed simple enough — but wouldn't it cause problems with the … what was the word? Where they all stood on the stage…

The blocking, that was it.

"You sure?" he said. "Won't we have to change all the positions round for the end of the scene and how will we—"

"Let's deal with that when we get to it, eh?" said Jez.

"Positions everybody, we've wasted enough time already tonight and I've got a rather important conference call I need to get home to — *capiche?*"

Graham hurried across to the other side of the stage. As he did, he saw Helen give him a quick thumbs up and mouth to him "You okay?"

He nodded back to her.

Even though she could sometimes be a bit pretentious, she always seemed to understand what he was going through.

In the wings, he looked out across the stage as Jez ran through the scene again. He followed the lines on his script, the action getting closer and closer to his own part, highlighted in yellow on the page.

Closer, closer, then the magic words from Helen herself: "If the Pearl of Bombay *has* been stolen then we shall never recover from the disgrace!"

He stepped confidently onto the stage and strode towards Jez.

Not a bad entrance, he thought. *Not bad at all...*

As he approached Jez, the director stepped back to give him room.

Graham looked quickly for his mark before remembering it would have to change now he was coming in from stage left — they'd just have to find him a new one.

He noticed Helen give him the slightest of nods and a secret smile. With new-found confidence he turned to Lord Blake, feeling for every moment like the local bobby, PC Bull, he was playing.

He drew a deep breath and heard his line echo around the theatre:

"Well then, well then. I hear there's been a crime committed."

He waited for Lord Blake to respond. But the line never came. Instead, from up in the rigging above his head, he heard the sound of a chain slipping.

And as he looked up in surprise he saw one of the heavy spotlights looming towards him from the darkness.

Graham went to move but too late.

The spotlight crashed into his shoulder, knocking him to the ground with an unbelievable jolt of pain.

AND WHEN GRAHAM next opened his eyes, two days later in hospital, that was all he could remember of his last rehearsal for *The Purloined Pearl*.

His plans for Ellie, himself — and his life as an acting policeman — destroyed by an accident.

One of his first thoughts, lying in the hospital bed … *It was only an accident, wasn't it?*

3.

A TRIP TO THE THEATRE

JACK PARKED HIS Austin Healey Sprite at the back of Cherringham Church and took the little path that led through the graveyard to the High Street.

As he walked he saw that the trees dotted among the graves were already full of pink and white blossom.

He could never get over just how damned *pretty* some parts of Cherringham were. Like every kid's story-book idea of an English village.

In spite of the bright sunshine he was glad of his winter jacket: there was a bitter cold wind. The cold — and the blossom — took him for an instant back to his time as a rookie cop in Manhattan.

Spring mornings in Central Park, banging his gloved hands together to keep warm, his breath hanging in the air, coffee and doughnut smells mixing with the scent of March flowers.

Well that was then, and this is now, he thought, turning on to the sidewalk and walking up past Sarah's office to the village square.

Everything changes.

Past Huffington's and the hotel, he stopped outside the newly renovated Cherringham Little Theatre. He looked at the place, painted a stylish white and grey. Steel and mirrored glass doors. A retro sign under the Victorian pitch roof.

Quite a transformation.

When he'd first arrived in the village the old building had been boarded up, its windows shuttered. A forgotten remnant of a time when villagers went out to films, shows, and plays. A casualty of the arrival of TV and then broadband.

But now it seemed people wanted the live experience back again. There was a demand for *real*. So, money had been raised, the builders had gone in, staff had been hired — and now, as he'd read in the local paper, Cherringham was just a month away from having a working theatre again.

The Cherringham Players were putting on an inaugural drama and the posters were plastered across the front of the building: *The Purloined Pearl — a Classic Mystery — guest director — internationally renowned Jez Kramer!*

Of course, in the last year Jack had seen plays, even a spot of opera in the village hall — but that didn't count. This was the real thing. This was show business come to the Cotswolds!

He pushed open the smart new doors and went in to the foyer. The place seemed empty.

Then he saw the tall double doors into what must be the auditorium swing open and Sarah and her mother Helen came towards him.

"Hi, Jack," said Sarah.

"Sarah."

Helen gave him a kiss on both cheeks.

"I'm *so* glad you're here, Jack, you are an absolute brick."

Over Helen's shoulder Jack could see Sarah smiling at him. She'd often teased him about how much closer Jack was in age to her mother — and hey, maybe you two should be the detectives?

But age didn't come into it. He liked Helen. But with her polite Englishness she was a different generation from him. Whereas with Sarah — he just felt... *comfortable.*

And now they'd worked more than a few cases together, they knew each other well.

"Glad to help, Helen," he said. "And I have to say — the theatre looks amazing."

"Doesn't it just? Let's do the grand tour," she said, taking his arm through hers and then lowering her voice, "Then we can get down to the nitty-gritty before the others turn up."

And into the theatre they went...

JACK STIRRED HIS tea and leaned back in the battered leather club armchair by the side of the prop fireplace.

Hmm, could do with a chair like this on the Grey Goose, he thought.

He smiled at Helen and Sarah who sat next to each other on a deep cushioned sofa. Helen had switched on just a few of the lights, so the stage had a cosy feel — not too different from the country house sitting room he supposed it represented.

"So..." he said. "Can't wait to see the first show. And I promise I'll buy tickets."

He saw Helen nod and smile.

"But — just what is the nitty-gritty we need to talk about, Helen? Sarah wouldn't tell me — said I should hear it—"

"From the horse's mouth, eh?" said Helen, laughing.

"Something like that," said Jack, sipping his tea.

He watched as Helen scanned the stage dramatically, making sure they were still alone. Then she started:

"We're under attack, Jack."

"We?"

"The Cherringham Players! Someone wants us out — and

13

I think they'll stop at nothing to achieve their aims."

Jack glanced at Sarah: *this for real?*

He saw her nod, her face serious. Much as Helen could be a little… *extravagant*… in her storytelling, Sarah clearly thought this was on the level.

"Since we started rehearsing *The Pearl*, it's been one calamity after another. Food poisoning, breakages, illness, thefts, accidents — I've never known a production like it. And now — well, I'm sure you've heard all about it — dear Graham Jones up to his neck in plaster. Literally!"

"And you don't think this is accidental?"

"How can a lantern fall on someone's head?"

"Lantern?" said Jack.

"Stage light, you know — spotlight — those things!"

She pointed above her head and Jack followed her gaze. Seeing the size of the lights up there he could understand why Graham was still in hospital.

The guy's lucky he's not dead.

"That must have been pretty bad," he said. "Were you here?"

"On stage with the poor chap. It was awful. Luckily the paramedics got here quickly and gave him some morphine."

"You saw it happen?" said Jack.

"We all did," said Helen. "Not that there was anything really to see. It just… fell."

Helen continued:

"But here's the thing. That whole lighting rig is brand new, top of the range — how can a big spotlight like that just fall?"

Jack shrugged: "Maybe that's the problem. New installation, teething problems, workers chasing a schedule. Wouldn't be the first time—"

"Nonsense!"

Jack paused.

"Well how about the police — what do they say?"

"Oh, we haven't bothered with the police," said Helen. "Alan Rivers, our intrepid local bobby? Good God, I used to hold his hand at playgroup when the older girls frightened him—"

"I think that's still happening, Mum," said Sarah and Jack saw her wink at him.

Helen laughed.

Nice timing, Sarah, thought Jack. *A little humour to calm Mom down a little.*

"Okay — nobody's called in the police. What about all the other incidents?"

"Taken one at a time, up until the light fell, they just don't seem that major," said Helen. "It's only when you add them all up, it doesn't make sense. To me, at least."

Jack looked at the two women sitting opposite. If it had just been Helen, he might have been sceptical. But Sarah clearly thought this was worth him hearing.

Then, as if she could read his thoughts:

"Something that Mum hasn't mentioned, Jack—"

He saw Sarah look at her mother — for permission? — and waited.

"Sarah, you know what I think about all that," said Helen. "Gossip. Tittle tattle."

"I think it's relevant," said Sarah.

"Oh, all right, go on then," said Helen.

"Well," said Sarah, "Word around the village is that the freeholder of the theatre — a local builder called Andy Parkes — thinks he's made a big mistake letting the refurbishment go ahead. Feels that — with the current market — he should have knocked the place down for flats."

"That happens," said Jack. "But now there isn't much he can do – is there?"

"That's it; apparently there is," said Sarah. "If the theatre can't demonstrate in year one that it has 'a credible business plan', then he can rescind the lease and take the building back."

"Wow, that's some small print," said Jack. "Who let that one through?"

"I don't like to name names, Jack," said Helen, "but unfortunately it's our Chair, Ambrose Goode. Ran the place for years, produced, directed, starred — but recently, well…"

"Ambrose is getting on a bit, Jack, and it turns out he's been rather in denial about his ability to keep on top of things," said Sarah.

"That's putting it mildly," said Helen.

"He insisted on negotiating the lease and only after it was signed did the other trustees see the sell-back clause," said Sarah.

"Ah," said Jack. "So if Ambrose is a little… flaky… I guess that's why you've got the celebrity director on the case — Jez Kramer?"

"Hmmph," said Helen. "It was the Board's decision. In my opinion, the less said about him the better."

"Ambrose and Jez don't quite see eye to eye," said Sarah.

"The man's poisoned the whole production," said Helen. "Him, and his ego. And he can be positively nasty, too!"

"Some of the cast have even walked out," said Sarah.

"Those who've been well enough," said her mother. "And the rest are at each other's throats as a result."

No fans of Jez Kramer here then, thought Jack.

"But anyway — he can't possibly be responsible," said Helen.

"No?"

"Well, it's hardly in his interest, is it?" said Helen. "He's being well-paid for his star-turn as director."

"Okay. So let's go back to the property guy — Andy Parkes. You think he could be sabotaging the show so the Players fail and he can get the building back?"

He watched Helen look pleadingly at Sarah. She clearly didn't want to say the words.

"I think Mum believes — it's possible," said Sarah.

"Not that I have any evidence. Still…" Helen said.

"Okay," said Jack. "Well, it's a theory. A motive — if nothing else."

"You think?" said Sarah.

"Sure."

"So what happens now?" said Helen.

Jack shrugged: "I like this little theatre. As a relatively new resident in Cherringham, I want it to succeed."

Helen beamed.

"Thank you."

"To start: we look for a modus operandi. Why don't you tell me exactly what happened — and show me how that lighting rig works?"

And Jack got up from his oh-so-comfy chair and walked into the wings.

SARAH SAT ON the sofa and worked on her laptop while Jack investigated backstage.

She'd spent all of yesterday afternoon getting feedback from a client on a website she'd built, and now she had to try and make sense of it all.

Plus — she'd never had a head for heights and she had no

intention of climbing up the little ladder into the lighting rig with Jack.

Once she'd made sure he was safety-clipped properly, she was happy to leave him to his devices.

For the last half hour she'd been able to hear him backstage, tapping away at metal, going up and down the ladder, moving chains around.

Had he ever investigated a crime in a New York theatre, on — what did they call it? — The Great White Way?

He certainly seemed comfortable in the theatre.

But apart from Jack's banging around, checking things, the building was silent. A haven. Her mother had been called home too, so in fact now — sitting in the middle of Lord and Lady Blake's faux drawing room — she felt quite at home.

I should come here more often, she thought. *Like working in Downton Abbey.*

She heard Jack coming down the ladder again and she watched as he emerged on to the stage wiping his hands with an old cloth.

"You find anything?" she said.

"Maybe," he said.

Sarah had learned to be patient when Jack was slowly working things out, but it did test her when he seemed to do it on purpose.

Almost teasing.

She watched as he stood in the middle of the stage and peered up into the darkness above.

"Yep, should work," he said, as if to himself.

Then he turned to her.

"Here's the thing. I want to try something out."

Sarah waited.

"And it could be dangerous. I might have got it wrong. I

could cause a lot of damage. God — it might cost a thousand bucks. Maybe more. An experiment that might tell us something."

"Then let's do it," she said. "Whatever it is you want to do."

"Such trust! Terrific," he said. "Now what I need you to do is hop off the stage now and head over there into the seats, just a few rows back."

"You're not kidding, Jack, are you?"

"Nope."

She went down the little steps at the front of the stage, walked up to row D then turned and faced him.

"Now — don't move. And if anyone comes into the theatre — shout out. Loud. Okay?"

"Okay."

"Because we don't want any more accidents."

She watched Jack disappear backstage for a few seconds then emerge again in the wings. He stood with his arms folded.

"Okay…" he said, speaking very slowly. "What I want you to do now is tell me exactly when you'd like one of those heavy lights to fall on to the stage."

"Really?"

"Really."

"You sure?"

"Sure."

Now she understood why he'd wanted her to stand in the stalls. But how could he make this work?

"How about…" Sarah waited, "Now!"

And as she said it, a huge sandbag dropped like a stone from above and landed with a massive thud on the stage.

It was like magic.

She looked at Jack. He hadn't moved an inch. He looked

19

pretty satisfied with himself.

"Wow," she said.

"Pretty good, huh?"

"What happened to the light?" she said. "That would have been fun."

"I was just kidding about the light," said Jack. "I was going to use a sandbag all along. Just as effective for a demonstration."

She climbed back up on to the stage and stood over the sandbag. She watched Jack as he joined her.

"All right, so tell me Mr. Houdini — just how did you do that?"

"Same way the killer did," said Jack, holding up a thin line of cord in one hand. "Unscrewed all the safety clips. Replaced the chain with this — on a slip knot. Hooked it somewhere backstage."

"So — he could just choose the moment — then pull the cord and the light would fall?"

"Yep. And nobody would even see him do it."

"No evidence left behind, either."

"Clever, huh?"

"But Jack. Hang on … you said — killer. Graham Jones didn't die."

"But that's it. If I'm right, I think maybe he was meant to. They got the timing wrong — or something. But whoever did it is playing hardball. And we'd better find them."

"Before someone does die?" said Sarah.

"Exactly," said Jack.

4.

A CALL ON THE DIRECTOR

SARAH PULLED HER SUV into the narrow driveway of the cottage that had been rented for Jez Kramer.

Barely enough room for the vehicle to squeeze through.

Backing out was going to be interesting.

Jez had eagerly agreed to meet Sarah, especially when she said she wanted to feature a profile of him for the next Cherringham newsletter.

Her real motive in meeting would — she hoped — not be too transparent.

She parked her car, pulling up close to a small garage at the back. The cottage looked perfectly maintained; beautiful paving for the driveway, warm Cotswold stone leading up to a slate roof.

She saw a pair of metal boxes attached to the side of the house. Air conditioning, no less. In Cherringham!

Not a bad cottage for the visiting celeb.

She walked to the back door and knocked, but Jez was already there, sipping from a teacup. He flashed a broad smile. She could feel his sharp eyes probing her.

He might have an ego; he might be pompous. But as an accomplished director, he could probably read people.

Jez Kramer took her all in.

"Sar-ah, good to see you. Come in."

Sarah followed him through the open back door. State-of-the-art kitchen, marble countertops, all the appliances, shiny stainless steel. A professional-looking Aga dwarfed the room.

No expense spared indeed.

She had to wonder if Kramer had demanded such amenities.

Air-con. Aga. Were there yellow and green M&Ms in a bowl in each room too?

Sarah realised that — since working with Jack — she had become more attentive to *seeing* things.

Then trying to interpret what they meant.

Like knowing that Kramer *didn't* have tea in his cup, but more likely whatever Winston Churchill used to have for his mid-day constitutional.

The expensive leather loafers, perfectly polished and smart. Savile Row for sure.

The shirt, from Pinks most likely. Beige, with subtle maroon stripes. Grey chinos, sharply pressed.

Altogether — Kramer very much looked the part.

Which is something he would be good at doing.

But Sarah had done her research. Kramer's career hadn't exactly been flourishing lately. Directing gigs like this were clearly tiding him over while the plum BBC drama projects went elsewhere.

"Come into the sitting room, Sarah. Rather a nice set up."

And he was right about that. Matching leather sofa and armchair; a dark wood floor that gleamed; two tear-shaped end-tables; a scattering of magazines on them, all part of the perfectly designed interior.

The fireplace — gigantic. You could roast a pig in it.

She sat on the sofa.

"Get you a drink… tea?" he tilted his own cup, with a wry smile. "Something stronger?"

She smiled. "No, I'm fine thanks, Mr. Kramer."

"*Jez*, please. Feel like I'm part of the Cherringham family, working with the locals, your charming mother."

She had the feeling that Jez Kramer didn't feel part of any Cherringham family.

Time for the interview.

She took out her pad and started asking some questions, all perfectly innocent and straightforward. To begin with, at least.

"WELL, YES, THOSE were golden days at the Beeb. Had my pick of projects, and the people I worked with? Absolutely the best."

"All different now?"

Kramer grunted. "You could say that — in *spades*. Controllers who wouldn't know a denouement from a divan. Young writers who don't give a damn about plot, or—"

He caught himself.

Then, the director quickly forced a smile onto his face, making his tanned, leathery skin criss-cross with wrinkles.

"Things change," he said, calming himself.

Decidedly unpleasant personality, Sarah thought.

Time to get closer to what she really wanted to talk about.

"And you too will take a role in the production?"

"Oh, yes, I mean the theatre board practically insisted!"

Sarah would have to check that with her mother, and see which way the "insisting" went.

"You'll be…?"

"Lieutenant Henry Collins. The dashing lover."

"Young lover?" Sarah said.

She just couldn't resist.

"Suppose. But it's not a terribly demanding role, so I can still direct. And for such a creaky piece of theatre as this, why not a bit of 'ham' to spice things up, hmm?"

She smiled at that.

Kramer looked away. "Besides, it's good to model for all the amateurs what it really looks like, this acting, taking control of the stage, eh?"

"Couldn't agree more."

Sarah flipped over a notebook page, as if moving on to another topic.

"Can I ask you about all these… accidents?"

Kramer was in mid-sip when he froze. A rather dramatic freeze, eyes narrowed, cup suspended in space.

"Why would you want to discuss any of *that* in your newsletter? Doesn't sound like profile material to me at all!"

He was coming at her hard.

But then, with Sarah's recent experience dealing with crime and Cherringham, she could — with a deep breath — take it in her stride.

"I'm sure that all our fans of the Little Theatre, and of the upcoming production — and your fans too — would love to be reassured that all is well."

Kramer nodded, thinking it over.

"My bobby is in the hospital, I've had the maid quit muttering about the theatre being dangerous after that food poisoning incident and we are just *weeks* away from opening night. So, how do you think I feel about all those accidents?"

Sarah nodded. Then her eye caught a small bureau in the corner, and a battered old trunk overflowing with papers and what she assumed were scripts. On a table beside it was a laptop and some gold and silver plaques.

Even from here, she could see they were citations… awards of some kind.

He actually travels with his awards, she thought.

Then back to the director — who she was sure was about to give her the heave-ho.

"No theory on the food poisoning, or the light that hit Graham?"

"Things happen, Sarah. We're all being extra vigilant now. Trust me; there will be no more accidents. And yes, that's exactly what they were."

She nodded as if Kramer's assurances were enough.

Then she pointed to the array of plaques.

"You have won some major awards. Mind if I…?"

She stood up.

This new direction clearly suited Kramer. "Oh, just a few things. To remind me of how high the quality bar can — and should be — held."

Sarah walked over to the bureau and picked up one plaque.

"A BAFTA?"

"Yes, for directing that series *The Fading Light*. The one about the returning soldier, Indian Army story, remember…?

"Gosh I certainly do. At school it was all we talked about. I think mum had a crush on the star — what's his name?"

"Hmm, well 'what's his name' is in his sixties now. You know, I still get fan mail about it, decades later. And—"

Kramer's phone trilled and he dug it out of his pocket. "Hel-lo? Tim? Good man. Was expecting your call, and… oh. I see. But I would still love to — oh, right. The producer's not in yet. Got it. Right. LA, sure."

Kramer nodded at Sarah a single finger in the air indicating that she need not rush.

After all, they were discussing Jez Kramer's brilliant achievements.

"I know. Traffic is crazy. Right I, well, I'll be here. Maybe this afternoon? Oh, okay. Whenever, then. 'All ears', as they say. By-ee!"

He quickly explained the significance of the call.

"New project for BBC America. Operating out of Los Angeles, can you imagine that? They could use a steady, experienced hand like mine at the tiller. So, yes——"

He did a good job of dissembling and hiding his disappointment at the visit that had obviously been deferred.

She guessed that LA and BBC America weren't summoning Jez Kramer to ride to the rescue.

Then he took a step closer to Sarah.

"Say, I just had a thought. That is, if you have no more questions."

Enough for now, Sarah thought.

"We're down a maid in the cast. Not an enormous role, but you'd be *perfect*. And, for your profile, you'd get to see me 'in action', as we say. Add a bit of 'colour' to the piece."

Sarah laughed. "I'm not really an actress, Jez. I think the last thing I did was play a shepherd in the Christmas play when I was seven."

"Listen. You look the part, and you speak well——"

This guy judges everyone and everything it seems, she thought.

"——I won't take no for an answer. Will you at least, think about it? A 'maybe'? We have the next rehearsal tomorrow night. I do believe that you'll fit the maid's costume perfectly."

She smiled, nodding, "Okay I will think about it."

He put down his teacup and clapped his hands together. Then — another unwelcome move — he gave her a big hug, probably standard behaviour among the directing/acting set.

"Fantastic. You will have a ball."

Based on what her mother had said, Sarah thought that was unlikely.

"As I said — I'll think about it," she reminded him.

"Yes, absolutely."

He guided her out to the kitchen and the back door.

"And do be careful reversing. Lovely cottage, but that horrible driveway was made for grocery carts, not cars!"

Then he opened the door.

"Thanks," she said, walking out to the still-chilly air, and the challenge of getting her Rav-4 out to the road.

5.

A CHAT WITH AMBROSE GOODE

JACK LAUGHED, SITTING in his parked Sprite as a light rain began to fall.

"He wants you to be the *maid*?"

Sarah was still laughing as well. "Yes. If only to get me to stop asking about the accidents."

He paused. Rain spatters hit the windscreen noisily. "You should do it."

"Jack — I'm hardly an actor."

"It could be fun, and besides, you see how your mother's worried. She'll feel better, you there."

"A maid?"

"You'll do great. Can't wait for the opening night."

"Hmm. Maybe I should remind him they need a replacement bobby too?"

"No way. With my accent?"

"And you're just going to pop in on Ambrose Goode?"

Jack looked at the cottage across the street.

Tiny, almost hobbit-like in size, with an untended spot of garden outside.

"Figured I'd surprise him. As former director of the company's shows, he might have a few choice words to say."

"Always seemed like a sweet man, Jack — but he is getting on."

"I hear you. I'll be gentle. Dinner at the Pig this evening?"

"Sure. Daniel is at his friend's tonight, and Chloe kind of comes and goes as she wants these days. She's involved in the school show, excerpts from *Anything Goes*."

"Great music — Cole Porter. And I know that 'coming-and-going' time. Suddenly they seem so independent, hmm?"

"Scares me a bit."

"Does everyone, Sarah. So... half-six for dinner?"

"Jack — it's okay. You can say six-thirty. I understand 'American'."

Another laugh. Sometimes just talking to Sarah made him feel good. He'd made many friends since he came to the village. But this connection with Sarah — and the detecting they did — made him feel like this could really be his home. *Far worse places than Cherringham,* he thought.

"Okay, rain's picking up. Let me pop in. See you soon."

And after Sarah's goodbye, he opened the car door quickly, and dashed across the road to the tiny cottage.

A SMALL OVERHANG barely kept Jack's head out of the now-heavier rain, and the back of his winter coat was getting soaked. Good in snow, but it wasn't at all waterproof.

I better start checking the weather, he thought. *English rain is nothing to ignore.*

His first ring didn't bring anyone to the door. Maybe Goode was out?

But then Jack heard the barking of what had to be a small dog with a high-pitched *yap*.

A voice on the other side of the door. "All right, Biscuit.

29

Easy now. Just the doorbell."

The dog, though, kept up its steady barking, and then Jack heard a lock being thrown and the door opened.

The man before him wore a quizzical expression, thin grey hair neatly combed to one side. Dress shirt, buttoned vest.

"Yes. What can I do for you? Not selling anything, are you?"

Jack shook his head, hoping that Goode would allow him entry out of the rain.

"Mr. Goode, I'm Jack Brennan, and—"

"That American fellow. New York cop, right?"

Goode's eyes had narrowed as he spoke.

Jack smiled. "You got it. And I'm friends with Helen Edwards."

"Good woman. Not bad at trotting the boards either."

If anything, the rain had gotten worse, but Goode seemed oblivious to Jack's state.

Jack nodded in the direction of the storm behind him. "You think I could come inside, just…"

Goode's eyes widened as though the thought hadn't occurred to him at all, opened the door, and let Jack in.

THE COTTAGE MIGHT have looked small on the outside, but if anything it felt even smaller inside.

Too much dark furniture, antimacassars turned a deep yellow from age. Had there been a Mrs. Goode who took care of such things, now gone?

Newspapers piled by an easy chair with an indented cushion. One light on in the gloomy room, windows covered by curtains that could make it hard for even a sunny day to penetrate here.

The dog — Biscuit — kept circling Jack, barking full out, a small dog –

And Jack liked dogs…

– but damned annoying.

"Biscuit, *do* calm down. Don't get many guests, Mr. Brennan."

"Mind if I sit?" Jack said.

Again, another thought that didn't seem to occur to Goode. But he made his way to his easy chair while Jack went to the couch.

Sitting seemed to calm the small mop-sized dog, and it scurried close to its master, and planted itself atop what looked like yesterday's *Guardian*.

"You said you're a friend of Helen's?"

Jack nodded. "Yes, and she's concerned about what happened to Graham Jones."

"Nearly bloody well killed. Close one, that."

"I can imagine. But the other incidents. People got sick from the first rehearsal dinner?"

"Days. Took me days to get better. Our maid, Alice, quit the show."

"I hear you might have a new maid?"

Goode looked up. "Really, and who—?"

"Helen's daughter, Sarah."

Another quizzical look.

"Really? Hmm — never knew she had any experience of theatrics."

Jack didn't offer an explanation as to why Sarah may have developed such a sudden interest.

"Tell me, you were the person who directed all the previous shows, yes?"

Goode's hands seemed to lock on the arms of his chair,

each ending in a wooden claw.

"Twenty years, Jack. We've done so many of the classics, *The Mousetrap*, *Major Barbara*, *The Glass Menagerie*, even *The Miracle Worker* with a working pump! All staged in that draughty Village Hall auditorium."

"Now you have this beautifully restored theatre—"

"And the Board bring in that pompous has-been, Jez Kramer!"

Goode raised his hand and pointed. "Mark my words, Jack. They will regret that. Mr. BBC, here without any of the talent propping him up that he's used to in London, trying to make a show come to life by badgering people."

"I gather you have no faith in him?"

Goode hesitated. "No. I don't. They'll wish that it was an 'Ambrose Goode' production by the time that mountebank is done taking their money."

"I hear he's cast himself in the play too."

"Ridiculous. Plays the young lover. At least I get the satisfaction of putting a bullet in him in the final act, ha ha!"

Goode paused, as if realising he'd gone too far.

"Metaphorically speaking, of course."

"Of course." Jack inclined his head.

No fan of the new director here either, he thought.

"And the spotlight accident…?"

Goode still seemed lost to his daydream about shooting Kramer. Then:

"Hmm? What it seems. An accident. In a theatre, new like that, things happen."

Jack nodded. *Accidents do happen.* But he also trusted Helen Edwards' instincts.

If she felt that something was wrong, it could well be.

"Ambrose, there's something else I was curious about."

The man's gaze finally came back to Jack.

Yes, Goode seemed a tad lost, maybe flaky. Jack could understand why the Board wanted to bring in someone from the outside. But he could also see why Goode would be so angry at that.

"Yes?"

Jack hesitated. Goode's mood didn't seem the best.

"It's about the lease you signed, for the theatre——"

After a long pause, Goode reached down.

On cue. Biscuit raised its head for a pat.

"What about it?" Goode said quietly.

"Seems like the theatre needs to turn a profit over the next twelve months or…"

Jack looked down at his notebook.

"…or Andy Parkes can reclaim the property despite it being a historical landmark. Tear it down if he wants. Put up flats."

Goode sat quietly.

Jack prompted him.

"That the deal?"

"Best I could get. At a monthly rent we could afford. I — I just assumed…"

"It would all work out. But if not?"

Again silence. Suddenly, Jack felt bad for the old-school director, here in his tiny cottage. A glance to the mantel showed a few pictures in dust-covered frames. But in the gloom Jack couldn't tell if it was a wife, kids, family…

It felt to him, that Ambrose Goode was all alone.

"Not the best deal, hmm?" Jack said.

Goode looked up. "I thought that the shows would all be packed, and with letting the theatre out for other events, to guest artists… we'd be fine."

"And if not, would you say that would all be to the benefit of Andy Parkes?"

"Yes. I imagine so. But I don't see what you're—"

"The accidents, Ambrose. Just thinking aloud, wondering who could benefit from such accidents, from the production being stopped?"

Now Goode leaned forward, eyes wide.

The guy hadn't actually thought about it at all.

"You're saying that maybe Andy Parkes might—"

"Hang on. I'm not accusing anyone. But if the accidents weren't just that, good to think who'd like to see *The Purloined Pearl* never open."

"That *bastard*."

Jack saw that Goode already had Parkes in — what did they call it here? — the dock, ready for sentencing.

He tried to calm Goode.

"It's what I do, Ambrose. Or what I used to do. Ask questions. May all still be an accident or two. But always good to know who has an interest in things going, as we say, 'south'."

Goode now looked away. If anything, this conversation seemed to have left the old-time director confused, even frightened.

Or — Jack thought — *is the director also a bit of an actor himself?*

Jack stood up.

"You're done?" Goode said, suddenly interested in more discussion with Jack.

"For now. Just trying to help out, Helen being worried and all. May have more questions later."

Goode struggle out of the chair, a great effort, Biscuit close at his heels as he came to Jack.

"Look, is there any way you can come to the rehearsals? If

someone is doing things, you'd be there to see them, catch them!"

"Be a little hard to explain to everyone."

Jack also had to wonder… was Goode asking this so that he knew what he was looking into?

"I don't think it would be appropriate."

Then Goode brought his right fist into his left palm.

"Got it! Our stage manager Todd Robinson, you know; the electrician? He's overwhelmed. Only his second show as full SM, and now with the new stage, lights, and all — perhaps you could assist him?"

Jack stopped.

Now that's an idea.

He'd certainly get to see everyone 'in action', as it were. Not that he knew anything about what a stage manager does.

"I really have never done—"

"It's just keeping props in order, getting sets and people in place, and you'd be there. I think it would give everyone a jolt of confidence — our own NYC detective in the house!"

Any more exuberance and Jack felt Goode would explode.

Jack laughed. "Okay. I'll do it. Maybe don't tell Todd the real reason I'm there."

"Great. No more accidents, and the show will go on. Huzzah!"

Considering how gloomy Goode had been when discussing the unfortunate lease, he certainly had turned it around.

"Tomorrow, seven sharp!" Goode said.

"See you then," Jack said, heading to the door, catching a glimpse through the bevelled glass windows of the old door that the rain still pelted down.

Note to self…

Always travel with an umbrella.

And he headed out, racing to his Sprite.

IT WAS WHILE driving back to the Grey Goose to get ready for his dinner with Sarah, that he had an interesting thought.

No matter if this all turned out to be nothing; he'd get to see his good friend playing the maid.

What fun, he thought, as he hit the road out of the village that led to the river, windscreen wipers struggling to keep up with the steady downpour.

6.

DINNER AT THE SPOTTED PIG

"JULIE, TELL SAM that this has got to be the best rack of lamb I've ever had."

Sarah saw the co-owner of the small restaurant beam. "I might tell him, Jack — but don't you think my husband's ego is already at bursting point?"

Jack laughed. "I imagine you're right." He took another forkful of the herb-encrusted lamb. "Our secret then."

Julie leaned down. "Glad you're enjoying it, and…" She turned to Sarah.

"The chicken is fantastic as well," Sarah said.

"Brilliant!"

Julie topped up both their glasses with a bit more Picpoul, and then moved on to other tables.

"I mean it," Jack said "This place, in Manhattan? You wouldn't be able to get a table."

On their first meal here — when was that, a year ago? — she and Jack had had a discussion about who was to pay. Sarah convinced him it had to be fifty-fifty, despite his protestations that he'd love to treat.

And though it was a splurge on her budget, getting out for a meal like this was indeed something special. And never a disappointment. Julie always gave them a corner table tucked away out of sight of prying eyes — and ears.

"So, looks like we're both part of the theatre company."

Sarah reached down to her purse and pulled out a folded stack of paper.

"Here's my part. I said 'maybe', but Kramer has me locked in already."

She watched Jack slip on his glasses to take a look at the pages. "Hmm, not a lot of lines."

"Good thing too."

He flipped through some more pages. "And seems that you're on stage when someone tries to shoot Henry Collins."

"Played by our good friend Kramer."

"The dashing young lover," Jack said, doing nothing to hide his sarcasm.

Then for a moment, he was quiet.

She prompted him: "What's up?"

Jack kept looking at the pages. "Dunno. Gunplay on stage."

"Just blanks, surely?"

Jack folded the pages back and handed them to Sarah. "Course. That would be the plan. Still — a little worrisome."

He sliced some more of the lamb, both of them trying to savour the phenomenally good meal, even though it would be easy to finish their dishes in minutes.

"So — good thing we'll be there, in the theatre."

Jack smiled. "Ah, so you are taking the part then?"

"Now they've dragooned you into helping too, it wouldn't be fair to refuse."

"After my little… *recce*… of the theatre, feel I know it pretty well. Could give Todd a hand, no problem. Long as Kramer doesn't try to cast me as the butler or the bobby."

"Bobby yes," Sarah said laughing. "But butler?"

"I know — a bit of a stretch."

"What do you think of what we've found out so far?"

"Not a lot to think on. Goode dislikes Kramer, to put it mildly. Andy Parkes is essentially waiting in the wings for the theatre to fail. As for Kramer, it would seem, with the state of his career that this has to go well, right?"

"I imagine so."

"If nothing else happens, then a pair of accidents have led us into becoming part of the Cherringham Players. Worse fates I imagine."

"Yes. You think—" She stopped.

Lately it seemed like her mind kept looking at events in different ways. She realised that when it came to bad things happening, she immediately became suspicious.

Probably because too often that suspicion has turned out to be justified, she thought.

Jack took another sip of the wine. "Go on."

"You think we should talk to Andy Parkes?"

"Maybe. Eventually. I think right now he might be taken aback. Though he certainly knew what he was doing with that lease. You know, I kind of felt bad for Goode. A bad deal — but I'm guessing he thought it was the only one he could get for the company."

"As I said, a sweet man. Had a wife years ago, and I think there are kids somewhere. But pretty much, these plays have been his life."

"And along comes the big-shot outsider."

"*Exactly*."

She saw the door open across the restaurant and Jez Kramer himself entered as if on cue, with another man.

"Speak of the devil," she said, touching Jack's arm. When

he looked up, she nodded towards the newcomer.

"Hottest table in town, I guess," he said. "Who's his date?"

Sarah watched discreetly as Julie took their coats and the two sat down. They hadn't seen her — but she now recognised Jez's guest.

"Pete Brooker," she said. "Stringer for the *Oxford Echo*."

"Theatre critic, huh?" said Jack.

"No," said Sarah. "And there's the interesting thing. He's News. Politics. Crime."

"Now that is interesting," said Jack. "Maybe we should stick around?"

"You think I need persuading? There's a pudding back there that already has my name on it."

Sarah knew, when it came to the Pig, passing on dessert simply wasn't an option.

7.

BEGINNER'S CALL

"GOBOS? BANJOS? TABS?" said Jack, laughing as he took off his heavy gloves and grabbing the offered mug of tea. "What kind of fiend invented all these crazy names for things?"

"You'll get used to it mate," said Todd, the stage manager, as he sat next to Jack on the props box. "Week's time, it'll all be second nature."

Jack looked around and very much doubted that. The morning had been a steep learning curve. One minute painting scenery, the next replacing electrical fuses, then working with Todd on cue sheets and rehearsal schedules.

Assistant stage manager. Definitely Jack of all trades, he thought.

But he loved the energy and sheer busyness of the place. Through the wings he could see out into the auditorium. The whole cast had been called this evening for rehearsal and he could see them now, dotted along the front row, chatting away.

Some he recognised from the village — some he knew well. There was the long-suffering Ambrose Goode, and a farmer called Phil Nailor who'd come in to replace Graham as the local bobby.

Sarah's mum Helen was chatting to an estate agent called

Laura who worked in the agency below Sarah's office. Jack looked at his cast list — Laura had the role of the drunken divorcee, Emily Cowell.

Next to them was his old friend Tony Standish, playing American millionaire suitor Ephraim Goldblum.

Ha! Now that is a performance I would pay double to see, thought Jack. Tony — Oxford-educated country lawyer — portraying a white-suited swain from upstate New York...

Backstage, other figures moved around, all caught up in mysterious tasks and chores, delivering props, dropping off paint, working on the big flats that were somehow going to be wheeled in and out when the scenes changed.

He hadn't realised it took so many people to put on a production like this.

"Hobnob?" said Todd, interrupting his thoughts.

Jack watched the stage manager reach deep into his overalls, pull out a small foil wrapper and open it to reveal a stash of biscuits.

Hobnob! thought Jack. *Might as well be speaking French.*

"Very kind of you Todd, but I won't," said Jack. "Pushed the boat out last night at dinner and these days — you know — gotta watch the calories." He patted his stomach.

"Tell me about it," said Sarah. Jack looked up as his detective partner passed by on her way to the stage to begin rehearsing.

"You wait till they deliver that maid's outfit, Sarah," called Jack after her. "I hear it doesn't take prisoners."

He watched her laugh and stride confidently over to the small group of actors he could just see through the curtains hanging at the side of the stage. He recognised Ellie from the pub — or 'The Honourable Clarissa' as he now should know her, since she got the part of Lord and Lady Blake's daughter.

Standing behind them with a hangdog expression was a morose-looking man with a bright green shirt and tatty jeans. Jack recognised him but couldn't quite place him.

He turned to Todd. "Who's the guy, looks like he'd rather be back home watching TV?"

"Oh that's Ben Ferris," said Todd. "Ha, I'll tell him you said that. He says people always tell him to cheer up and it drives him absolutely mad."

"He a regular?"

"Been doing this longer than I have," said Todd. "Works at Costco's packing shelves. He's playing Hobbs, the butler."

"You know, one thing I am glad of — being back here with you and not out there in front of an audience."

Todd grinned at that. "Me too! You never acted at school then?"

"Third grade was the very last time," said Jack. "Opening night of the Christmas play, I totally forgot my lines. Froze. Deer in the headlights. Nobody helped me out — so I just walked."

Todd laughed. "What, you mean — you actually left the stage?"

"Yep. Didn't stop. Walked right past the other kids. Into the wings. Along the school corridor. Out of the fire exit. And straight home."

"Well, you won't need to do that here," said Todd. "When they finish rehearsing, I'll take you through all the cues again, give you some homework."

"Appreciate it, Todd. And thanks for the tea."

Jack handed his mug to Todd — but instead he watched Todd hand his own back to him.

"I made 'em," said Todd with a grin. "You wash 'em up. House rules."

"Gotcha," said Jack, smiling back.

"See you over at the lighting board, all right?"

"Be right with you."

Jack watched him turn and go. He was going to like working with Todd — about as straightforward as they came.

He picked up the mugs and headed through the wings, and down the little flight of steps into the corridor.

But as he turned towards the kitchen door he felt a sharp jab in his ribs.

"Stick 'em up, pardner and turn round nice and slow," said a male voice in a cartoonish American accent.

Words that would have given him pause on a New York City street.

But here, Jack turned and smiled. Facing him, grinning and holding a large revolver which Jack had to believe was a prop — was the director — Jez Kramer.

"You're not from around here, are ya *fella?*" said Kramer.

"Hello," said Jack. He could see that Kramer was disappointed that his little game was going to end.

"You see what I did there?" said the director, letting the gun dangle from his hand. "Not from around here? Because — well, you're not, are you?"

"That's true," said Jack. "And also obvious."

Kramer stuck out a hand, and pumped Jack's. "Jez Kramer." Kramer kept inspecting Jack, his eyes slow like a lizard's. "Jack, right? Ambrose told me he'd got you on board to help out," the director said, accent banished.

"He said you'd be happy with the arrangement," said Jack. "I hope you are?"

"S'pose so," said Kramer. "So yeah, of course — very happy, good to have you aboard. All hands needed on deck for this creaky barge of a play!"

Kramer looked around for someplace to put the gun. And Jack reached out for it.

"D'you mind?"

Kramer handed the gun over for Jack to examine.

"Smith and Wesson .38," said Jack, releasing the cylinder then clicking it back into place. "Real thing, huh?"

"So, I'm told," said the director. "Little memento of one of my *dramatic successes*. Given to me by a grateful cast and crew. Re-tooled so it can only fire blanks, of course."

"Really?" said Jack.

"You're the expert."

"Not anymore."

"I imagine you used to carry one of these."

"Long time ago… and far away."

"We must have a drink sometime. Share experiences of the Big Apple. Love the place."

"Sure," said Jack, not meaning it. He handed the gun back.

"Anyway — I'd better get on with things here. We're rehearsing the big scene where I declare my undying love for the Honourable Clarissa," said Kramer.

He leaned in with a smirk and Jack could smell whisky on his breath: "Though in real life I'm not sure how, er… *honourable*… our Clarissa is, if you know what I mean."

Jack didn't respond. He decided to let the snide comment about Ellie ride — for now.

But he made a mental note not to forget it.

Kramer frowned, then turned to head back to the stage area. As he did, Jack placed his hand on his arm.

Firm but friendly, Jack thought. *Enough to make him think.*

"Just one thing, Jez," he said, smiling. "Appreciate it if you never point that thing at me again — okay?"

Kramer looked confused and blinked nervously — then his

bluster returned.

"Sure thing, *pardner*. Accidents happen. No more gunplay, hmm? You have a nice day, now."

Jack watched him go. No wonder Kramer had put everyone's back up. The guy was a grade-A asshole, no mistake.

He picked up the two mugs and headed down the corridor. But just as he reached the small kitchen area in the back, he heard a piercing scream from the main auditorium.

He put down the mugs, turned — and ran back towards the stage.

SARAH CLAMBERED DOWN the steps of the trap and into the space below the stage.

In the darkness she could see Ellie lying motionless on her back.

She kneeled down next to the young woman then placed her hand on the floor so she could lean forward to check her pulse. She felt her palm slide through a sticky wet pool.

Oh, God, she thought. *Not blood, please…*

Then she realised it was just the tea from Ellie's shattered mug which lay next to her.

"Hey, Sarah," said Ellie, suddenly opening her eyes and starting to get up.

"Whoa! Don't move Ellie, you might have broken something," said Sarah, reaching out for Ellie's hand.

"God! That was some fall," said Ellie brightly. "But you know what? I do believe I got away with it."

Sarah could now see Ellie's face clearly, grinning.

"Okay, but don't try to get up quite yet — let's check first."

"Hey Sarah — you all right?" came Jack's voice from

behind her.

Sarah turned in the cramped space and saw Jack scrambling down the ladder from the stage to join her, a big torch in one hand. Up above him, she could see the faces of the rest of the cast crowded round the trapdoor, peering down.

"I'm fine," she said. "It was Ellie who fell."

"You think you broke anything, Ellie?" said Jack. "How did you land?"

"On my backside if you must know, Jack," said Ellie, laughing. "And fortunately I've got a lot of padding."

"Nothing hurts?" said Sarah.

"Apart from my pride," said Ellie. "I bet it looked bloody funny though."

"Not to me," said Sarah.

"What happened?" said Jack.

"One minute I'm running across the stage into 'my true love's' arms — next minute I'm falling through a bloomin' hole in the floor!"

"Someone must have opened the trap?" said Jack.

"Second she stepped on it — the thing just folded open," said Sarah.

She saw Jack looking up at the trapdoor mechanism.

"Let's see if you can stand, shall we Ellie?" said Sarah. "I still can't quite believe you're not badly hurt."

"Down the Ploughman's we've got a hole down to the cellar — I've lost count of the number of times I've gone arse over tit down there. Honest — I'm okay."

Sarah looked at Jack and tried not to laugh. If Ellie was unharmed then it was a big relief.

"Come on then," she said.

And she and Jack helped Ellie to her feet.

"Everything all right down there?" came Ambrose's voice

from above. "Ambulance is on its way."

"Hey, I don't need an ambulance," said Ellie, brushing herself down. "But I'll tell you one thing. This top'll never come clean."

"You should see a doctor anyway, Ellie — just in case," said Jack, helping her up the steep steps. "And somebody ought to stay with you this evening."

"Totally agree," said Kramer, his face suddenly appearing at the edge of the trap. "I'll look after you. Nothing's too good for our leading lady!"

Hands reached down from above to help Ellie up on to the stage and Sarah watched carefully to make sure she didn't fall back again.

"It's a very kind offer, Jez," said Sarah quickly. "But I'll make sure she gets home okay and put her to bed."

"Oh," said Kramer, clearly disappointed at the lost opportunity. "Right you are then."

As Sarah looked up through the trap, the other actors disappeared from view to care for Ellie. She turned to Jack.

"I don't believe in accidents any more, Jack."

"Me neither. That fall could have killed her."

"Could have — or should have?"

"Maybe. You head up top, take care of Ellie. Reckon rehearsals will be over for tonight."

"What will you do?"

"Get Todd to join me down here would you? On the quiet?"

"You think someone tampered with the mechanism?"

"Sure of it."

"I'll see if I can place where everyone was when it happened."

"Good thinking," said Jack. "Catch you later?"

"Why don't you drop by in the morning. Have breakfast with the kids."

"Will do," he said. "Oh and Sarah — you be careful, okay? Whoever's doing this just doesn't seem to care who's in the firing line."

Sarah nodded to Jack and climbed the steps. It was going to be a long evening.

8.

HOT NEWS

"BACON SANDWICH ISN'T a bacon sandwich, Jack, unless it's got HP in it."

Mouth already half-open, Jack stared at Daniel who was thrusting a small bottle of sauce at him across the kitchen table.

"HP, huh?" said Jack, putting his bacon sandwich down on his plate and contemplating the mysterious bottle.

"Don't listen to him, Jack," said Chloe. "That stuff's disgusting."

"Yeah? What do you know?" said Daniel to his sister.

"Leave him be, both of you," said Sarah coming in with a pot of coffee and putting it on the table. "Freshly brewed Jack — in your honour."

"Appreciate that," said Jack. He took the bottle of brown sauce, poured a little on his sandwich and ate.

He could see Daniel watching intently, waiting for a verdict.

"Interesting," said Jack.

"*Knew* you'd love it," said Daniel, grabbing his coat and bag then heading upstairs.

"Don't forget your lunch, love," called Sarah.

Jack watched Chloe grab a piece of toast and walk out of the room.

"Manners, Chloe. How many times—"

But she was gone again. Jack heard the front door slam and guessed that she was racing off to school.

They come... they go.

He loved this chaos though — took him back twenty years to New York, breakfasts at home, everyone flying out the door.

"Sorry Jack, she's just—" said Sarah.

"Hey, no worries. I have a daughter, remember?"

Daniel came racing back into the kitchen.

"Football kit mum!" said Daniel.

"Where it should be," said Sarah.

Jack watched the twelve-year-old trying to compute the notion that something might be located where it should be — then caught Sarah's eye as Daniel stormed back upstairs.

Sarah sat at the table and poured them both a coffee, then waited. Jack could hear Daniel slamming cupboards open and closed...

...then he heard him race down the stairs again.

"See you later Mum, bye Jack!" shouted Daniel.

And then Jack heard the front door slam and there was silence.

"So," said Sarah, sipping her coffee. "Where were we?"

Jack pulled the morning's paper from his jacket and handed it over.

"Page five," he said. "You can't miss it."

He watched Sarah leaf through the pages, then stop abruptly.

"*Cherringham's very own Ghostbuster — Hollywood director Jez Kramer shrugs off attack of the spooks in real-life theatre mystery*," she read.

"See the picture?" said Jack.

"Oh, very classy," said Sarah. "Mr. Kramer himself with his head underneath his arm."

"I suspect that's just where your mother would like it to be, huh?"

"Her and a lot of the cast too," said Sarah, still reading the article.

"Gets worse," said Jack. "Someone's even unearthed a connection between the theatre and Mabb's Farm."

"*Brave director battles ancient curse and accidents to bring forgotten masterpiece to public attention,*" read Sarah. "Maybe time to page our local mystic, Tamara, hmm?"

"Interesting spin on events."

"And totally made up."

"Don't forget — it is a newspaper."

"Listen to this — *"'I may have won many BAFTAs," says Jez, "but I do so believe in giving back — little theatres like Cherringham can benefit from my professional experience.'"* Yuk."

"You see the by-line?"

"Umm… Oh. Of course. It had to be."

"Your very own pal we saw in the restaurant — Pete Brooker."

"Written the day *before* Ellie's accident, I bet," said Sarah, tossing the paper on to the kitchen table.

"Over a nice meal at the Pig and a few single malts afterwards Jez Kramer, no doubt." said Jack.

"So — you think Kramer's behind all this? Sabotaging his own show to get publicity?"

"I wouldn't put it past him," said Jack. "Those famous BAFTAs were a long time ago and right now I'd say you're seeing a career on the rocks."

"But if he was behind it all — how? He's been on stage

every time there's been an accident."

"Maybe that's the plan — he's got a ready-made alibi."

"You're thinking he has an ally? Someone in the cast pulling strings?"

"Literally," said Jack. "Whenever an accident happens, our hero's right there in the thick of it."

"But Jack — everybody hates him. Why would anyone help him?"

"It's amazing what a few hundred bucks can do to change an opinion."

"Maybe," said Sarah. "But what about the trapdoor yesterday? I saw him walk across it twice in the scene and nothing happened."

Jack thought about that.

"Hmm. I gotta say that's the one thing that doesn't quite add up. Unless his partner-in-crime was below the stage all the time waiting for a cue to set the trap."

"Sounds complicated," Sarah added.

Jack nodded. "You're right," he said. "Whoever did it had slipped two of the four bolts and left all the hinges in place."

"So there's no way they could predict when it would give way?"

"I don't think so," said Jack. "It was totally random. Ellie just got unlucky because she raced into the scene and hit the trap hard enough."

"Wait — then it could just as easily have been Kramer?"

"Unless he avoided the spot, waiting for someone else to fall through."

"So where are we? Could Kramer really be doing all this, just for the publicity?"

"Maybe. I'm not taking our beloved director out of the frame," said Jack. "Just thinking we need to dig a little deeper down at the theatre."

He watched as Sarah opened up a folder that lay on the table and took out the details of the cast and crew.

"Let's make a list," she said. "Who's got a motive? And who can we place at the scene of the crime?"

"Gotta love lists," said Jack. "But don't forget — could be more than one bad guy."

"Okay," said Sarah, sliding her finger down the cast list. "I'm going to take out Tony and my mum — okay?"

Jack laughed at that. "Sure."

"Which leaves, starting at the top: Ambrose?"

"He's certainly got a motive. But I doubt he could fix the trap door, or climb up to rig the lighting."

"Kramer?"

"Well he's obnoxious and ambitious enough, though in a court of law that doesn't mean much."

"Ellie?"

"Unlikely — but if we are talking about anyone who might possibly be a suspect, don't rule her out. I hear she's always short of cash."

"You're a suspicious man, Jack Brennan," said Sarah. "Laura?"

"Estate agent huh? Could be a stooge. Maybe working with Andy Parkes…"

"Hey! Now you're just getting personal. Laura's sweet. How about Phil Nailor?"

"Hmm, our new stage bobby. Real-life farmer, so he could fix the ropes and bolts for sure. But no motive that I can see."

"And — he wasn't even around for the first rehearsals."

Jack poured himself another coffee and pondered.

"Hey, I know," said Jack. "The butler did it!"

"You mean — what's his name, guy who works at

Costco's?"

"Ben something."

"Ferris," said Sarah. "Possible — but motive? I don't think so."

"That all the cast?"

"Save for me. Should I be on the list?"

Another laugh. "I'll vouch for you. Hmm, okay... How about backstage?"

"Well apart from you — and against my better judgement I'm likewise sticking you in the innocent pile — there's just Todd."

"Again, no motive I can see," said Jack. "But he's certainly got the expertise. The trap, the light... could be a motive we don't know. Yet."

"And you like him."

"I do," said Jack. "But that shouldn't get in the way."

He watched Sarah fold up the cast and crew list.

"That's everyone, Jack."

"Plus our property developer."

"Andrew Parkes," said Sarah. "Why don't I track him down for a little chat today?"

"Why not? Then, let's you and I see who's looking guilty at tonight's rehearsal. Start asking some questions."

"You not going to finish your bacon sandwich?" she said, getting up and starting to clear away.

"I think not," said Jack helping her take the plates to the dishwasher. "No offence — but maybe next time I drop by for breakfast you hide that evil brown sauce from Daniel?"

"Let me guess — you're a mayo man or nothing, huh?"

"You got it," said Jack, putting on his coat. "See you tonight Sarah."

And he headed out.

The skies looked clear, and if it didn't rain, he had plans to give the Grey Goose — the Dutch barge he lived on down on the river — the beginnings of a spring clean.

Nothing like scrubbing the decks for solving a crime…

9.

TEMPERS RISING

SARAH WAS LATE getting to her little office overlooking the village square, but she knew her assistant Grace would have opened up and got the coffee going.

When she opened the office door though, she got a jolt of surprise: there was a man standing at her desk facing her.

For a second she thought she'd disturbed an intruder.

"Who are you?" she said instantly, looking quickly round the office for signs that Grace was there.

Then Grace came out of the little kitchen at the back looking nervous.

"Name's Parkes," said the man making no move to shake hands — or smile.

"Andrew Parkes?" she said, confused. Why was the man she'd been planning on speaking to today here now?

"The very same."

Grace stood motionless at the kitchen door: "Sorry, Sarah, I told him he couldn't come in without an appointment but he wouldn't go, just *insisted* and I didn't know what—"

"That's okay, Grace, not your fault," said Sarah, taking off her coat and not removing her eyes from her visitor.

"This is a busy office, Mr. Parkes, how can I help you?" she said.

"Busy huh? World I live in, we start work at eight," he said in a monotone. "Guess you city types just swan in when you feel like it?"

"As Grace told you — we usually only meet clients on an appointment basis."

"Yeah, but I'm not a client, am I?"

"So how can we help you?" said Sarah, horribly aware of the current of aggression that marked Parkes's every word. She looked quickly over towards Grace — her assistant looking just as concerned.

"You can start by explaining why the hell you're slandering me all around the damn village?"

"I don't know what you're talking about—"

"Telling people I've been causing accidents in the theatre, hurting people, poisoning and the like."

"What? I've done no such thing—"

"Sticking your nose into my business and looking at my contracts — which are private — do you understand the meaning of private?"

Sarah for the first time in a very long time felt scared — this guy was seriously angry, she and Grace were alone up here in the office, and his whole body language was barely restrained fury…

Got to stay calm, she thought.

"Mr. Parkes, I have done *none* of those things, and I'd really appreciate it if you'd just calm down—"

"Don't you bloody tell me to calm down, woman, this is my livelihood."

Sarah nodded to Grace in a way they'd practised before — a way which meant *call the police now* and she was relieved to see Grace slip away into the back kitchen with her mobile.

Parkes stepped forward.

"I'm the only builder round here putting up houses for the people who live in this village — right? People who put in a day's graft. Social housing, not bloody galleries or fancy shops or theatres so people from London like you can rip us off and put up prices, and you — you — you've got the cheek to start investigating my business? You — and that bloody Yank who should go back where he came from — you two, all you've done round here is cause trouble—"

"Mr. Parkes! We have not investigated your business and I am not slandering you. I was told about your deal with the Cherringham Players and it is public knowledge. All I am trying to do is find out who is causing trouble at the theatre. Now if people are saying you stand to gain if the place fails that is not a rumour I have started—"

But Sarah could see nothing was going to stop him.

He started to advance towards her and instinctively she stepped back.

"You'd better watch yourself, little miss detective, I've got powerful friends round here, just you see."

"Don't you *dare* threaten me."

Parkes was really close now, his breathing fast, his words hissing at her: "One word from me and I could get you closed down — running a detective agency, where's your planning permission for that, eh? You mention my name once more, or I hear you've been asking about me and I'll—"

"What exactly will you do then, Andy?" came a man's voice from the door. "I'm interested to hear this. Go on. Tell me."

Sarah turned to see Alan Rivers, the local policeman, his big frame filling the space, his uniform suddenly so reassuring.

Sarah saw Parkes take in the situation and step back.

"All right, Alan?" he said, still breathing heavily.

"Had a complaint there was a disturbance up here," said Alan calmly, but Sarah could see he meant business.

"No disturbance," said Parkes. "Just — a little disagreement."

"That right, Sarah?" said the policeman.

Sarah took a deep breath. The moment seemed frozen as she realised nobody quite knew what to do next.

"Mr. Parkes was just going," she said.

She watched Parkes shake his head.

"Yeah, I'm going. But don't you forget what I said."

At the door he stopped, still blocked by Alan.

"You're in my way — *officer*."

Sarah saw Alan look to her, but she shook her head. Alan stepped to one side and Parkes disappeared down the stairs.

Sarah stepped back and sat against one of the desks. Grace hurried over from the corner of the office and the two hugged each other in relief.

"Jeez," said Sarah. "What the hell just happened then?"

"What a bastard," said Grace.

"You all right, Sarah?" said Alan, coming over.

"I am, now you're here," she said. "How come you were so quick?"

"I was just over the road in Costco's when Grace called," he said.

"Grace, sweetheart — you were brilliant," said Sarah.

"I was terrified," said Grace. "But you looked so cool!"

"That might be how I looked," said Sarah. "It wasn't how I felt."

"You want to stay clear of Parkes," said Alan. "I knew him at school. He fights dirty."

"Tell me about it," said Sarah.

"Who fancies a tea?" said Grace. "Alan — you staying for one?"

"Sure."

Sarah watched Grace head to the kitchen then turned to Alan.

"Do you think he's going to come back?"

"No, not now he knows I'm involved," said Alan.

"He did threaten me, you know — or at least, he threatened the business," said Sarah.

"Well, that's something you probably should take seriously," said Alan. "He's got the Parish Council wrapped round his finger and people tend to do what he wants."

"Why?" said Sarah.

"He brings work and money into the village. Lot of people rely on him."

"When you say he fights dirty...?"

"We've never pinned anything on him."

"But?"

"Off the record — I think he uses other people to do his house-keeping, if you know what I mean."

"Got it. So we should be careful."

"If you and Jack are sniffing round his business, then yes, Sarah. You should be very careful indeed."

Grace returned with a tray and started pouring the teas.

And Sarah thought to herself how dangerous her little detecting side-line could be...

10.

THE PURLOINED PEARL

JACK STOOD OFF stage right, which he noted, looking out to the theatre, was on his *left*.

Something important to remember — as the actors gathered in the centre of the main set, the drawing room of the Blake Manor House.

Jez clapped his hands as if summoning school children.

"All right, people — circle around. A few notes before we run through this big party scene."

The actors gathered closer to Jez.

"You all know your marks. Todd has reassured me that the trap door is secure so — no more tumbles down *that* rabbit hole."

"Thank God for that," Ellie said. "My bum couldn't stand another crash landing."

The actors laughed but Jez didn't even respond, Jack saw.

"Hopefully we're done with accidents and can focus on the play because we all know -"

Ambrose Goode grunted and finished the sentence.

"The play's the thing."

Again, Jez paused.

"Precisely. So then, any questions?" Kramer didn't give

more than a second for a response to that. "Okay then, places — and we begin!"

The actors went to their appointed spots on the drawing room set.

Todd came beside him. "Okay to just watch?" Jack asked the stage manager.

"Until we do the light change at the end of the scene — but for now, enjoy."

And together they watched the Cherringham residents morph into highly dramatic characters from a century ago.

AMBROSE GOODE WALKED away from the fireplace, a 'brandy' in his hand.

"A toast to all who join us on this auspicious occasion."

He raised his glass.

"I second that," estate agent Laura said with a tad too much slur, even for the drunken 'Emily Cowell'.

Jack watched Sarah and Ben Ferris, maid and butler respectively, circle the group with trays of glasses filled with tea as stand-ins for brandy.

Sarah looked decidedly uncomfortable, Jack thought. Not that he'd ever tell her.

And the butler? Even more so. Was he *supposed* to be acting disgruntled?

"Hang on," Kramer said taking a step forward from a nearby bookshelf.

He shifted from his acting role as the 'handsome lieutenant' to director.

"You two — maid and butler, can we get some smiles, *puhlease*? It isn't a wake after all. And Sarah, a bit of a curtsy perhaps? And the butler, a little bow? God, don't you people ever watch *Downton Abbey*?"

Sarah nodded. Taking direction from Jez Kramer was not going to be easy.

A nod from Ben Ferris as well.

"And Lady Blake," this to Sarah's mum Helen, "You are not happy with the way things are going, so stay back a bit. You're hardly going to smile, are you, hmm?"

"Yes," Helen said.

Another clap of hands. "Okay then, from where we left off. The toast, please — with feeling!"

Ambrose Goode took a few steps upstage (the front of the stage, Jack had just learned).

"To my beautiful daughter, Clarissa ... I wish her the very best in the years to come, as Lady Blake and I announce her imminent—"

"Stop!"

Kramer put down his own glass and walked completely upstage and turned.

At this rate, it was going to be a long night.

"Ambrose," he said slowly. "You do know that this is your only offspring, yes?"

"Of course," Ambrose said.

"And you are announcing her upcoming nuptials to the dashing army lieutenant, Henry Collins?"

"Dashing. Bit of a stretch, that, don't you think?"

The company laughed.

Uh-oh, Jack thought.

Kramer walked over to Ambrose Goode, still grinning from his joke at Kramer's expense.

"You are currently delivering that line as if announcing the grand dairy livestock winner at the Royal Highland Show." Another step closer. "She's not a 'cow', Ambrose, she's—"

Kramer looked over to Ellie, as if delivering a genuine compliment, "A ravishing beauty, the apple of your dim-witted eyes, an absolutely spectacular jewel…"

"I delivered the lines as directed."

"You delivered the lines *precisely* the way someone with your lack of talent, wit and understanding would. Like a stick that talks."

And that was that.

Goode took his glass, and in a jerky motion tossed the tea right into Kramer's face.

"You pompous, ridiculous…" Ambrose seemed stuck for the right word.

The cast had backed away from the tussle, as if not sure what to do.

Jack looked at Todd, who shrugged.

Maybe such things are supposed to happen in a theatrical production? he thought.

But the dripping Kramer reached out and grabbed the much older Goode by the lapels of his sport coat.

"You *fool*. You talentless village bumpkin. No wonder they had to replace you. The only role you're fit for—"

Kramer was shaking Goode around now and the level of physicality ratcheted up a notch with each shake.

"—is the village idiot."

Goode seemed unmoved by Kramer's shaking and Jack winced as the older man suddenly slapped Kramer in the face.

"Ha!" shouted Goode as Kramer froze. "Taste of your own medicine you pompous little twerp. You can take your BAFTAs and stick them—"

But to Jack's amazement Kramer rallied and launched himself at his producer with a roar, scattering the rest of the cast.

"Nobody talks to me like that!"

Jack saw Sarah shoot him a look.

Maybe not in the stage manager's job description but…

Jack ran over and quickly pulled the two of them apart.

Kramer acted as though he was struggling against Jack, but Jack could feel that the struggle was more for show.

Goode, meanwhile, looked as if he had got out of the lift on the wrong floor at Harrods.

Ellie came over to Kramer with a small towel, and the director, calming down, wiped his face.

"He's *fired*."

Which is when Sarah's mum Helen took — as they say — centre stage.

"Jez, Ambrose my dear man… we're all a little edgy. With everything that's been happening."

All eyes were on Helen, almost as if she really were Lady Blake.

"We have only one day to dress, then the first performance." She turned to Kramer. "*No one* can be fired."

Jack guessed that Kramer could take that to mean for himself as well.

"Jez, you are the director. But I think you might phrase things a little more… diplomatically."

Kramer held his tongue.

He obviously didn't want the production to end.

Newspapers were publishing articles about him!

"And Ambrose, we have performed in so many great productions together. Can't you give this one your absolute best? We all know how wonderful that can be."

Goode hesitated for a few moments, then nodded. "Yes. I suppose so."

"Well, as a Theatre Company board member, I am so

terribly glad to hear that. Now, maestro…"

A little needle there? Jack did so like Sarah's mum.

"Perhaps we might resume the rehearsal?"

"Yes. All right — places as before. The toast please."

He delivered an exaggerated smile to Ambrose Goode, "If you would be so kind?"

Then, as if noticing that Jack was still there. "And can we *please* clear the stage?"

"Right," Jack said.

He hadn't expected to be breaking up brawls today.

And as he walked back to the wings, and the rehearsal began again, he had to wonder what other surprises lay ahead.

11.

THE PLAYERS AT THE PLOUGHMAN'S

"READY?" TODD SAID to Jack who had his hands on the curtain ropes. "Your cue is when I flash the lights on stage, two times, then we go dark and—"

"Curtain."

Todd grinned. "Precisely. Least that's how Kramer wants the act to end."

"And what Kramer wants…"

Jack turned back to the stage. It was the end of the party scene, leading to a big moment. No more fights had broken out, and except for a roll of the eyes by Ambrose and the occasional exasperated look from Kramer, things had gone smoothly.

Then the plan — for those who wanted it — was a post-rehearsal retreat to the Ploughman's.

Hopefully, without the director in tow.

"What you are about to witness…" Goode, in character, said, holding a dark mahogany case, "is a most precious article that few have seen since I brought it back from the hot, mysterious city of Bombay back in ninety-four."

The actors formed a near semi-circle around "Lord Blake" and his mysterious case. They pretended to look at each other with curiosity. This play, Jack knew, was written in 1912.

And it sure felt like it...

"As a reward for service to King and Country, the Royal Indian family of Jain, long the wealthiest family in the land, presented it to me. For services rendered, of course."

More "oohs-and-ahhs" from the actors.

Then:

"And on this, the occasion of my lovely daughter Clarissa's engagement being announced..."

Now both soon-to-be-newlyweds, Ellie and Kramer, turned to the group and smiled.

"I wish to present this great prize to my daughter and for all her heirs, in perpetuity!"

"All set?" Todd whispered.

Jack nodded.

Goode seemed to have some trouble holding the mahogany case up with one hand, while his other went to the front to open the lid.

"Bit of a tilt," Kramer said through his clenched-teeth smile, slipping in a tiny bit of direction.

Goode kept his smile on as well as he tilted the case more towards the theatre, then slowly pulled on the case's top.

"Ladies and gentlemen, I give you... The Pearl of Bombay!" Goode said, in what must have been as loud a voice as he could summon. Then, scanning the group whose smiles had now been replaced with horror-struck looks, eyes as wide as could be.

There was nothing there, save the velvet nest for the pearl.

"My God! It's been *stolen!*" Goode — the thunder-struck Lord Blake — said.

The stage lights flashed as if a lightning bolt had exploded over the room.

Once… twice…

Then the lights cut out completely, and Jack quickly lowered the curtain.

The act, and the rehearsal was over.

And nobody got killed, Jack thought.

ELLIE HAD WALKED into her usual place behind the bar of the Ploughman's and suddenly the soon-to-be-married Clarissa vanished to be replaced by the familiar cheery barmaid.

Todd stood next to Jack.

"What can I get you, Todd?"

"Hmm, think I'll have a Stella."

Jack turned back to Ellie. "Make that two pints of Stella please, *Clarissa.*"

It almost felt that — with the rehearsal ended — people just continued in their parts as they walked over to the pub.

Sarah sat with Tony Standish whose broad American accent in the show would be sure to get laughs — even for the lines that weren't actually funny.

And Sarah's mum had come to the pub, sitting at a table with Ambrose Goode — maybe doing some damage repair on the guy's ego.

Kramer had passed on the pub gathering.

Probably wanted to preserve his aloof status as the artistic "visionary" of the show, thought Jack.

Also Laura — aka the tipsy divorcee in the show — had begged off, saying she had a long drive home. And Ben Ferris, who didn't say much save for the lines in his script, simply vanished.

Ellie put down the two pints.

"Thanks," Jack said.

That first sip... *not bad.*

"So, Jack," said Todd. "You enjoying it so far?"

"Sure. Fun to see the thing come together."

"And the fight refereeing?"

Jack shook his head at that. "Let's hope that's done with."

"Dunno. That Kramer — he's got under everyone's skin. Good thing I just work backstage or we might, as they say, 'have problems'."

"Hear you on that."

The pub wasn't crowded; the actors making up about half the patrons. Quiet night.

Not a bad time to talk and ask some questions.

"Todd, the things that have happened. That light falling, the food poisoning, the trap door—"

"Close one that! Our girl Ellie here could have really hurt herself."

"Yeah. That's what I mean. What do you make of it all?"

Jack looked at the electrician, someone who seemed solid as a rock. But Jack had said to Sarah that really anyone can go on the suspect list, suspicious, that is, if these weren't all a string of strange accidents.

But Todd?

It would be a giant leap to think he had anything to do with the things that had happened.

"Okay. Here's the thing Jack. I helped set up the stage lighting. I mean, I'm a bloody competent electrician, aren't I?"

Jack smiled. "So I've heard."

"Right. And I can tell you, they were secure, all properly bolted, the rigging perfect. And then — one falls..."

"People talk to you about it?"

"A few. Natural, that, isn't it — wanting to blame someone. I mean, they *know* I set them up. But—"

He turned to Jack, pausing for a moment to make sure that his next words were out of earshot of anyone but Jack.

"Someone must have tampered with that light, Jack. It was no accident."

"You sure?"

"Absolutely. Those things were locked in. I'd put my own mother under any one of them. Someone *did* something."

"No accident?"

Todd hesitated. "Could someone have gone up there to take a look at the lights, maybe knocked one loose? It's not impossible. But the question is…"

"Yeah?"

"Who? And why?

"Classic questions," Jack said, "Least in my line of work."

So Todd was as suspicious as he was. But that prompted an additional question.

"If you thought someone tampered, weren't you worried?"

Todd nodded. "Sure. Maybe someone wanted to hurt the theatre now that it's back in full swing. Maybe they didn't want to really hurt anyone, just scare them. But Jack… see, these are my people, my village."

Todd looked away. This was a side to him that Jack hadn't expected to see.

Then he looked back. "If someone's out to hurt one of our own, I can do more good being there than not."

"Feel the same way myself. Even though this isn't exactly my village, my people."

Todd's smile returned. "They sure the hell are, Jack. You kidding? You're practically our NYC Mascot."

Jack laughed.

It was good to know that there was an extra pair of watchful eyes on the stage. Especially with the big dress rehearsal to come. Anything could happen.

He saw Tony Standish stand up and fire off a "goodnight" wave to everyone, leaving Sarah on her own.

Exit Stage Left, Jack thought.

"Think I'm going to catch up with Sarah a bit."

"Yup, and my missus will be wondering where I am anyway, Jack. See you tomorrow."

Jack nodded and walked over to the back table.

"SEAT FREE?"

"Been saving it for you," Sarah said with a smile.

Jack sat down. "Don't think I've ever seen your mom down here at the Ploughman's."

"I *know*! Doesn't seem quite right, does it?"

"Lady Blake with a half of lager. Now that's what I call fitting right in."

Which brought them to the topic of the rehearsal.

"Jack — sorry you had to get between those two. Can you believe it?"

"Good thing that they were more bluster than muscle. Still, no love lost between them."

He nodded at Ambrose, embroiled in deep conversation with Helen Edwards.

"Ambrose there, and Kramer."

"Still — we got through the rehearsal, the pearl being 'purloined' and all. Maybe we're over-reacting. Could be they are all accidents, and—"

Jack stopped her with a nod.

He told her what Todd had said about the lights.

And he himself had found a way it could have been triggered.

"So," he said. "No accidents. Least Todd's on our side. Watching things."

"Not a suspect?"

"Was he ever?"

"Which leaves…"

"Pretty much everyone else. Not that we have anything. Really, as we get closer to performance, I'll be worried."

That stopped Sarah, her eyes on Jack's.

"What do you mean?"

"Whoever is doing these things — why would they stop? And what better time to strike than just when the show is coming together?"

"The first performance?"

"Or maybe even sooner, when everything is in place, all the actors, the props…"

"Final dress rehearsal? Jack — you're scaring me."

He was tempted to tell her not to worry.

It's all going to be okay.

But Jack was anything but sure of that.

"We need to find out more. And we're running out of time."

"There is one thing, Jack," said Sarah. "Maybe it's not important."

"Everything's important."

"Well, you know the estate agents down the stairs from my office?"

"Sure — the one Laura works in, no?"

"Yes. Grace remembered that last year — when there was all the fuss about the theatre being turned into flats — Andy Parkes was in there nearly every day."

"Interesting."

"Maybe Laura knows something," Sarah said. "How about I speak to her?"

"Okay, except — *I'll* talk to her. Let Parkes come after me if he gets upset again."

"You're right. In which case, I'll take on Ben Ferris."

"Our butler?"

"Yes. So quiet, but he's been with the company for a while. If nothing else a chat might eliminate them both as possibilities."

"And otherwise, we... *you*... need to be careful, on that stage."

Sarah nodded. Then he saw her look away. "Mum's done, looks like. I'm her ride home."

Jack turned. He saw Ambrose Goode navigate his round body out of a wooden chair that he had been barely able to fit in, and walk gingerly to the pub door.

Guess it's been a few years since he *was in a punch-up,* thought Jack. *If ever.*

Helen walked over.

"Ready, Sarah?"

"Sure." She turned back to Jack. "I'll call Ben tomorrow morning."

She was aware her mother was listening. But Sarah knew Helen, more than anyone, wanted to find out what was happening.

"Great, and I will pay a visit on our 'divorcee'. See what her connection to Andy Parkes may be—"

"Oooh, he's a nasty one," Sarah's mother said. "Unscrupulous as they come."

"And in my country," Jack said, "they come pretty unscrupulous." Then, to Sarah: "Catch up tomorrow? Before the dress rehearsal?"

Jack felt that Helen wanted to ask questions — but she held back, letting them go through their process.

"Goodnight, Jack," Helen said.

"Goodnight."

And Jack stayed sitting there.

Thinking... *just as the play builds to a climax, could these events be building to something?*

Something deadly?

Could he and Sarah figure out what that was in time? Who might be behind it?

And the one question that he kept coming back to...

Why?

12.

THE BUTLER SPEAKS

BEN FERRIS MERELY mumbled when he answered his phone, as if immobilised by this unexpected call.

Sarah's mother had all the numbers of the cast in case of an emergency, so it had been easy for Sarah to reach him.

But talking? That was another story...

She had explained what she wanted to speak to him about — and Ferris said that he was "too busy".

Too busy stocking shelves at the local Costco? she almost said.

But instead she explained that she and Jack had been talking to everyone. And wouldn't it look odd if he, Ben Ferris, wouldn't talk?

When Ferris finally agreed to meet at lunchtime, Sarah thought it would be where he lived — his address a tiny flat in the village, above the bookshop.

But he quickly said "No."

Then: "And not at that coffee house," he said. "Bunch of busybodies work there."

She thought of the bookshop below his flat that Sarah hadn't been to in months... with a new owner and new name, "The Book Cottage."

When she mentioned that possibility, he hesitated.

"Ben — it will just be for a quick chat," she added.

Then, not hiding his reluctance, he said, "Okay. In ten minutes."

Now, the call ended and taking a breath, Sarah put her computer to sleep and turned to Grace.

"Going to The Book Cottage," Sarah said. "Shouldn't be gone long."

Grace nodded, carrying on with her work, as Sarah got up from her desk, and headed for the shop.

A BELL OVER the door jingled as she entered.

The small shop, specialising in quality used books as well as the newest releases, looked empty.

But then the owner, new to Cherringham, a small, rotund woman — Rosie McHugh — came out of a little room at the back, a smile on her face.

"Hello," the shopkeeper said. "Can I help you?"

"Hope so. I hear the new Archer is a great read. And—"

"All sold out of that one, I'm afraid," Rosie said. But then she came out from behind the counter. "Michael Connelly has a new one, getting *great* reviews."

The woman pointed to a neat line of the Connelly novel on the top shelf of new releases.

"Thanks. Might be just the ticket." Sarah took a look around at the otherwise empty store. "I'm also," Sarah said as she slid the novel out, "meeting Ben Ferris here. In minutes, really. You know him?"

A nod, and then, finally a smile. "I do indeed. The upstairs tenant! Haunts this place. Limited funds but always checking out what's new."

"Quite the reader, then?"

"Oh, more than that. Quite the *writer*. Always checking out the books about writing, plays, novels. Last week he picked up *The Selected Letters of Elia Kazan*. You know, Mr. Ferris once wrote professionally!"

No, I did not know that, Sarah thought.

Just thought he was quiet Ben Ferris, working his hourly wage job, struggling to get by.

But a writer?

"No, I didn't, I—"

And at that moment the bell over the door trilled again, and Ben Ferris walked in, face set, a nod to Rosie McHugh, and just a stolid look for Sarah.

Sarah smiled and went over to him.

BEN WASN'T TERRIBLY good at eye contact.

He led the way back to where there were shelves devoted to books on writing and writers' biographies. As Sarah asked him questions, her voice low, Ben would slide out one book, then another.

"Ben, I wanted to know your thoughts about what's been happening in the theatre."

He paged though the book in his hands, bent over, and then slid it back in, pulling out another.

"You mean the arguments and stuff?"

"Well, yes." Sarah paused. "That and the accidents.

"Accidents happen."

"You mean you think there will be more?" she asked.

He looked up at her.

"I don't know. Do you?"

"You think someone could be doing them on purpose? That they aren't accidents?"

"Anything's possible."

Like pulling teeth here, Sarah thought.

She moved on.

"And that fight between Jez and Ambrose."

"Idiots," Ben said.

"For fighting?"

Another look up. Ben Ferris weighing every word.

Then the tiniest of smiles. "Sure."

But Sarah wasn't sure at all.

Ben had been a fixture in the local productions for years. She wondered what he thought of an outsider coming in, so now she asked him.

Ben slid out another book.

Sarah could see the title. *The Trip to Echo Spring.*

After a long pause, Ferris said: "Guess the Board thought old Ambrose wasn't quite up to it."

"And you?"

Ferris shrugged. "Always seemed to do just fine before. Maybe they wanted…" He slid the book back in. Buying new hardbacks on what passed for a Costco salary couldn't be indulged too often, Sarah imagined.

"Look," Ben made a point of looking down at his wristwatch. "I'm due back at work in twenty. So, gotta dash."

Sarah nodded, thinking that this just may have been one of the most useless "interrogations" in her short career as a sleuth.

Ben Ferris started walking to the front of the shop, heading for the door.

When Sarah amazingly remembered a line from an old American detective show.

The detective's *gimmick…*

"Oh Ben — just one more thing."

The guy stopped and turned, halfway to the front desk.

Nearly free of Sarah's questions.

"Hmm?"

"I hear you were a writer. That you wrote professionally."

For the first time she saw a spark of reaction in his eyes.

She half expected him to shake his head and walk away. Instead, he slowly walked back to her.

Almost theatrical in the way he took each measured step.

His eyes never leaving hers.

"Who said that? Rosie?"

A nod from Sarah.

"Can't tell anyone anything these days, right?" Ferris said, a thin smile on his lips.

"So it's true?"

The smallest nod. "Yes, I was a professional writer. With all the wonderful moments that profession brings, all the joy, all the—"

He stopped.

"Can I ask what you wrote? Who did you write for?"

The thin smile faded. "It was years ago. I wrote for myself. Like every talented writer, every real writer who isn't a hack."

"What though?"

"Stuff. It was another life, Sarah Edwards, another world."

He clearly wasn't going to tell her anything more about that "other life". But there was obviously more to Ben Ferris than she had assumed when setting up this meeting.

And while he might not want to talk about that other life, Sarah knew that, these days, one's past never vanished.

If nothing else than for her own interest, she wanted to find out just what Ferris had written.

"See you at dress," he said, the thin smile returning.

Sarah stood there for a moment and let Ben Ferris walk out.

And when Rosie McHugh, who had diplomatically busied herself in a back area, still probably within earshot, returned, Sarah said, "You know, I think I'll get the Connelly. Could use a good read."

"Absolutely," Rosie said.

Now paying for the book, she wondered how Jack would get on when he met Laura at the estate agents that afternoon...

13.

LIAISONS DANGEREUSES

JACK ARRIVED AT the theatre dead on four p.m. and thought at first that he'd got the call time wrong: although the doors were open and the house lights on, the place seemed empty.

But as he walked down the central aisle towards the stage he could hear voices from out back.

Raised voices. People quarrelling.

He stepped up on to the stage and nearly bumped into Todd who was standing in the wings eating a burger.

"All right, Jack?" he said, his mouth full. "Fancy a chip?"

"Not hungry Todd — but appreciate the offer."

"Not going to get much chance to eat tonight."

"I'll figure something," said Jack, nodding to the corridor. "What's up?"

"Laura and Jez," said Todd. "None of my business."

Jack nodded. "Right. Well, nothing to stop me from grabbing a coffee."

And he set off through the wings and down the corridor towards the kitchen.

So this was where Laura was. He'd phoned the estate agents earlier and been told she was off sick.

Doesn't sound sick now, he thought as he approached the kitchen door, the raised voices at full throttle.

"You selfish *bastard*—"

"Sweetheart, I just say it how it is."

"Get out of here."

"One day you'll look back on this and realise how right I was."

Jack heard the smash of a plate or cup — hard to know which — and stepped back just as the door opened and Jez Kramer hurried through and past him towards the stage.

"Beginners' call in an hour Laura, don't forget," the director hurled over his shoulder.

"Bastard!"

Jack waited a few seconds then tapped on the kitchen door.

"Hi Laura," he said gently. "Jack here. Safe for me to come in?"

There was no answer so Jack entered, ready to dodge more crockery if it flew his way. But as he entered the little kitchen he could see Laura sitting at the table blowing her nose on a paper handkerchief.

"Mind if I grab a coffee?"

"No. G-go ahead."

"Want one?"

"Sure."

He filled the kettle, waited for it to boil then made the drinks and handed one to Laura.

"Sorry about that," she said. "One of those days."

"So I gather," said Jack. "I called you at your office today, but they said you were home, sick."

"Yeah. Truth is I had a bit of personal stuff to sort."

"Our beloved director, huh?"

"Hmm."

"I didn't realise you and Jez were…"

"We're not. I mean, we were. But now we're not."

"Right."

Jack waited for her to say more, but she clearly wasn't going to.

"So Laura… The reason I wanted to talk to you was — Andy Parkes."

"From one bastard to another, huh? What do you want to talk about him for?"

"I gather your office was helping him with his development plans for the theatre?"

"What is this, Jack? What are you talking about? That stuff's confidential — how do you know about that?"

"Whoa, it's all right. I'm just trying to make some connections here. All the accidents we've been having. Things aren't looking good for the debut of the theatre. And some people are wondering if Parkes might be involved."

"And if he was — you think I'd know? And not say anything? Give me some credit."

"Sure. I understand."

"If you must know, my company did some valuations of this building for him. But I wasn't involved."

He stood back as Laura suddenly got up. "I've got to get into costume."

She brushed past him toward the door.

O-kay, I handled that well, thought Jack. But then to his surprise, she stopped at the door and turned.

"Do you know what really pisses me off about him?"

"Parkes?"

"No, Kramer. The fact that he thinks I'm so bothered by him that I'd break into his house."

"What do you mean?"

"Someone turned his cottage over this afternoon," she said. "Smashed everything up."

"And he accused you?"

"As if I care enough about him to do that. I mean — truth is — he's just some old has-been, isn't he?"

Jack watched as she shook her head in disgust and walked away.

Suddenly there was a lot to think about. Laura and Kramer? How had he and Sarah missed that? And a break-in. What the hell was going on?

14.

AN UNEXPECTED SHOCK

SARAH HADN'T FELT like this since she was at school. Excited, nervous, thrilled — but also part of a team.

She looked around the Ladies' Dressing Room and knew now why her mother would never give up her amateur dramatics or the choir.

It was just such *fun*.

Seated in front of a line of mirrors and light bulbs down one whole side of the room were the other female members of the cast, laughing, giggling, helping each other with hair and make-up: Ellie, Helen, her mum, Laura.

Someone had brought their iPhone and had plugged it into a big speaker — their party playlist was blasting out.

All around her, other female friends and relatives of the cast were bustling around, sorting costumes, caught up with the rhythms of the room and the music.

She looked at herself in the mirror and had to laugh again.

Whoever had ordered the maid's costume had clearly selected it from the sixties comedy film section: far from the demure Edwardian outfit she'd expected, it was low-cut, black with white lace trimmings and with a short skirt.

"Hey Sarah — better not wander round the village

wearing that," said Ellie, "or you'll get yourself arrested."

"Hmm, maybe she wants to be," said Laura, teasing. "The strong arm of the law eh, Sarah?"

"Just you and Alan Rivers up at the police station — now there's a thought," said Ellie, laughing. "Him in his police uniform, you in your little maid's outfit—"

"Ladies please, no more!" said Helen in her most outraged Lady Blake voice.

"That's a life sentence in itself," said Sarah, joining in the laughter. "Now, where's my feather duster?"

The room collapsed into giggles and then all the lights went out and the room was thrown into total darkness.

"Whoa!"

"What happened?"

"Don't panic—"

"Hang on, I've got my phone,"

As Sarah turned on her own phone light, other people flicked on phones and torches too.

"What's going on?" said Laura.

"Power cut, I guess," said Sarah.

"There should be some emergency lanterns in the cupboard there," said Helen.

Sarah watched as the lanterns were pulled out and switched on. Suddenly the raucous atmosphere had gone.

"Let me have one of those," said Sarah grabbing a lantern. "You lot stay here, and I'll go see what's up."

SARAH STEPPED OUT through the dressing room door: a dim orange light from the street lamps outside the theatre spilled into the corridor giving it an ominous glow.

She could hear voices from the stage, so headed down the

corridor, holding the lantern high. She carefully climbed the little steps and walked through the darkness into the wings.

Through the drapes, Sarah spotted a small group of people on the stage, some of them holding torches and emergency lights.

They were crowded around a figure lying on the ground.

Another accident? Who was it?

Let it not be Jack, she thought with an unexpected feeling of dread as she hurried forward...

Then she felt a hand on her shoulder.

"Whoa, Sarah," came a voice. "It's all right."

She spun round — Jack stood there with a torch in one hand.

"Jack," she said. "Thank goodness. What's happened? Who is it?"

He gently pushed her lantern to one side. "It's okay. It's Todd . Electric shock — knocked him across the stage, but he's going to be fine."

"I thought it might have been you."

"Could easily have been."

"How did it happen?"

"He was testing the Christmas lights. You know the scene where Lieutenant Collins—"

"Jez Kramer,"

"Yep, Jez Kramer. The scene where he turns on all the lights to surprise everybody at the party. Anyway, Todd just flicked the switch and it blew in his hands."

"You think someone sabotaged it?"

"Normally I'd say let's wait for forensics. But here? After all the other accidents? I'd say it's a dead certainty."

"The perfect trap," said Sarah. "And whoever did it could be anywhere right now."

"Exactly," said Jack.

The lights suddenly came on again throughout the theatre and Sarah could hear muted cheers from the dressing rooms.

She switched off the lantern and put it down.

She could see Todd now being helped to his feet by, on one side, Phil Nailor, the replacement bobby, and on the other, Ben Ferris in his butler's costume.

The electrician stood to his full height, brushed himself down and gave a cheery 'thumbs-up' to her and Jack where they stood in the wings. She saw Ambrose give him a good pat on the back then lead him away backstage.

Ben and Phil stood examining the string of party lights which had all blown, but Kramer wasn't having any slouching around it seemed: he moved centre stage, clapped his hands and shouted "Excitement's over. Back to work everybody, beginners' call in twenty! No excuses now!"

"The show must go on," said Sarah. She looked at Jack who was peering at her, his face confused. "What's wrong?"

"That's some outfit."

"You think I'll get away with it?"

"I think you'll get an encore all on your own."

"Not exactly *Downton*'s dress code."

"Well yes, but the play *ain't* exactly Shakespeare either, let's be honest."

Sarah saw Kramer approaching.

"Come on now, Jack, Sarah, we need to clear the stage please," he said as he passed them.

"You know, Mr. Kramer — if Todd hadn't tried that switch first you'd have been the one lying on the ground there?" said Jack.

Kramer turned and stopped: "That fact has not escaped my notice, Jack, but one learns in this business not to dwell on the 'what ifs'."

Sarah could see that for all his blustering confidence Jez Kramer was scared.

If this was all a set-up to grab some press attention, perhaps it wasn't going as smoothly as he'd intended.

Or perhaps he really was the target...

"And sorry to hear about your break-in," said Jack. "I hope nothing of value was taken."

"Ah the babbling gossip of the air," said Kramer, his voice rising an octave.

Break-in? thought Sarah. *Things are happening faster than I can keep up with.*

Kramer seemed to be waiting for a response but as neither she nor Jack gave one, he clearly gave up on the rest of what must be a quotation: "No, nothing was stolen. As far as I can tell. Whoever it was contented themselves with trashing the place."

"That's awful," said Sarah, meaning it. "All of those personal things that you brought with you? Your prizes, photos...?"

"Especially those, it seems," said Kramer. "But thank you for your kind thoughts. And now — we have a show to put on."

Sarah watched the director hurry away.

"Lonely guy," she said.

"I wouldn't count on it," said Jack. "Seems he and Laura have had a little fling."

"You're joking," gasped Sarah, genuinely astonished.

"And a little bird down the Ploughman told me he made a play for Ellie too."

"Yuck."

"Word is she told him where to get off."

"Good for her."

"But you know, Sarah — we missed all of that."

"You're right," she said. "I wonder what else we've missed?"

"Soon as this rehearsal gets under way, I'm going to head out to Kramer's house, snoop around a little."

"You think the answer's out there?"

"Break-in? Can't be coincidence."

Sarah watched Ben appear from the wings carrying a tea tray. He placed it on a small table then exited through the other wings.

Sarah suddenly remembered she hadn't fed back to Jack after her meeting with Ben.

"Speaking of coincidence. Turns out our butler used to be a writer."

"Really?"

"Guess writers don't go round all the time looking like Oscar Wilde or Hemingway. But still — working at Costco?"

"I know. Doesn't fit." said Jack. "What kind of stuff did he write?"

"Well, that's the funny thing. Did a little digging. He wrote some theatre when he was pretty young. Shifted into soaps for a year and then just... gave up."

"Did he say why he stopped writing?"

"Wouldn't talk about it at all," Sarah said. "I found some scattered credits, lot of gaps and nothing more recent than ten or fifteen years ago."

"Maybe he just burned out? Happens, I guess."

"But to end up working in a supermarket — that's so sad."

"He's not exactly over-endowed with people skills, Sarah," said Jack. "Maybe he couldn't hack the personal stuff. You know — agents, meetings..."

"Maybe," she said. "Anyway, I'd better get ready, I'm an opener. Spend the whole scene cleaning the fireplace, then I get the killer line 'will that be all, Miss?' and exit stage left."

"Give it everything you got Sarah — next stop Broadway."

"Don't be gone too long Jack, will you?"

"I won't," he said. "And you be careful, huh? Could be we haven't seen the last of these 'accidents'."

Sarah left Jack to check on Todd and headed back to the dressing rooms. Her mother had been right to ask for help all those weeks ago.

Suddenly it seemed like the whole cast really were under attack.

15.

AND THE WINNER IS...

JACK PARKED A hundred yards up from Kramer's rented cottage and strolled down the lane trying his best not to look like a burglar on his way to a break-in. He nodded and smiled at an old lady who was mowing her front lawn.

She nodded back at him but didn't smile.

Guess I do look suspicious, he thought.

He knew he didn't have much time. He hadn't been able to get away from the dress rehearsal until well into the first half, which, according to Helen's timings gave him less than an hour before he was needed for a big scene change in the second act.

With luck there wouldn't be any more "accidents" while he was gone.

He reached the cottage and strolled up the driveway, then slipped into the porch by the little back door.

It only took a minute with his special lock-picks — a handy relic from his NYPD days — and he was in.

The old cottage was dark, with small windows, but he wasn't going to turn any lights on. He scanned the kitchen. Kramer had clearly left in a hurry — dishes piled high, teabag on the table. A half-empty bottle of Scotch.

But no sign of a break-in. Maybe the star director had made it up? Bit of attention seeking?

Then he went into the sitting room — and saw straight away that this was no story. Furniture had been slashed with a knife, glass broken, vases smashed. Papers and books were scattered everywhere, surfaces cleared, pictures torn from the walls and destroyed.

Whoever had done this had to have been in a frenzy of anger. Or maybe they were just disguising the true nature of the break-in?

Jack reserved judgement until he'd looked around a little more.

He started with the papers. Hundreds of torn pages of typed script scattered around the room like confetti. Jack realised they were the remnants of TV scripts, ripped from their binders and flung everywhere.

Some of the pages were covers — and on them he could see titles of old British TV shows with dates going back into the nineties.

He picked up an award, broken in two. Heavy glass. On it the words *Royal Television Society — Best Drama Serial — The Fading Light.*

Sarah had told him how *The Fading Light*, written and directed by Kramer, had held the nation gripped when she was still a girl at school in Cherringham. The story of Britain's bloody retreat from the Empire in the forties. A tragic soldier's tale, it had made Kramer's name and launched the career of so many of Britain's biggest TV and movie stars.

No way would Kramer have destroyed this award.

It represented the high point of his life. This break-in was for real. So why?

Jack put the smashed plaque to one side and approached

an old trunk, which lay on its side. The lid had been wrenched back and the contents spilled. More papers, but also props, pictures, photos, scrapbooks.

This was clearly the mother-lode: Kramer's personal effects, the memorabilia of his long career in theatre and TV. Jack began to go through the pile.

He sorted through faded newspaper articles, reviews of long forgotten shows.

Pictures of Kramer as a young actor before he became a director. Photos of Hollywood stars that Jack recognised. *Variety*, the *Hollywood Reporter*, a wry headline "The Brits have come — and now they're going!" with a cartoon version of Kramer himself underneath.

More scripts in tatters, and then—

Jack stopped dead in his tracks.

He reached down and picked up the ragged front page of a script. There was no mistaking the title:

The Fading Light — First Draft.

But it was the words underneath that threw everything into sharp focus:

By Ben Ferris
What?

The surly shelf-stacker at Costco's — the original writer of one of the country's greatest pieces of TV drama?

Jack sat back on his haunches, trying to fit it all together. The years matched with what Sarah had told him about Ferris's career — the soap writing then the sudden withdrawal from the business.

Had Ferris written this story, then somehow had it stolen by Kramer? Rewritten? Jack knew that in Hollywood such tales were legion — writers and directors "disappearing" from shows they created, fired, bought out — but did it happen here in genteel England?

Was this Ben Ferris's revenge? To destroy Kramer's little theatre show? It didn't make sense. The accidents which had happened in the theatre weren't damaging Kramer in any way — they were just undermining the theatre and everyone's hopes for its success.

There had to be something else.

Jack reached over and pulled at the old trunk until all its contents poured out. A stack of ancient DVDs spilled across the wooden floor. Jack looked at the titles — all shows from the eighties and nineties that Kramer had no doubt directed.

Including the box set of *The Fading Light*. He picked it up and read the small print on the back — no mention of Ben Ferris. Written and Directed by Jez Kramer.

As he was about to throw the box back into the trunk, his eye was caught by an image on the cover.

A dramatic moment from one of the episodes. The hero — he guessed — a young soldier, pointing a revolver at the chest of a pompous looking general... and about to pull the trigger.

Jack looked hard at the image. That revolver. A Smith and Wesson .38 — exactly the same type of gun which Kramer was using in the production.

Coincidence?

No such thing as coincidences.

The gun had to be the same one. And twenty or thirty years ago, the rules were a lot looser when it came to de-activating weapons for props. Chances were Kramer had been lugging this gun — a memento — around all this time without ever checking if it had been made safe.

But where would he have kept it?

Jack scrabbled around in the wreckage of the room, looking for a clue — anything — that might be connected to the gun.

He found it. A small polished wood case with an inscription on the front — "To the boss from the Cast and Crew: keep hitting that target!" He opened the case — the inside was lined with velvet.

There was the space for the gun — and next to it a slot for ammunition.

Empty.

Then he thought of his own gun case back home, and lifted out the velvet tray. Scattered in the dusty base were the remnants of cartridge boxes bought over the years: Remington, Winchester, Federal...

One or two of the bits of cardboard said "blank cartridges".

But most of them just had the words: .38 special.

Live rounds.

So Jez Kramer was lying when he said the gun had been made safe. He used it himself — what for? Drunken party games? Showing off?

Whatever. It looked like someone had broken into his house and just stolen Kramer's live rounds.

Someone with a big-time grudge.

And now, with a seamless opportunity to commit a murder — one final "accident".

With a sick feeling in his gut, Jack knew the perfect time for that accident... in the big scene at the end of the play, when Lord Blake turns his gun on the dashing lieutenant, putting a round into his body.

He remembered the pleasure with which Ambrose had described shooting Kramer in that scene.

Blanks or not, Ambrose would be sure to aim at the heart.

And with the bullets stolen — if Jack was right — Ambrose wouldn't be firing blanks.

Tonight he'd be firing live rounds.

Jack reached for his phone to ring Sarah to warn her.

Then he remembered: final dress rehearsal, all the phones would be off.

The only way to stop this murder was to get to the theatre in time. He checked his watch.

If the rehearsal had gone to schedule, then the curtain would be coming down in twenty minutes.

Twenty minutes to save a life.

Jack turned and ran.

16.

STAGE VILLAIN

SARAH MOVED TO her place at the side of the stage, standing next to Ben Ferris — whom she now saw in a completely different light.

Meanwhile, Ambrose Goode was making the most of the play's final moments, leading up to the big confrontation between Lieutenant Henry Collins and Lord Blake.

A case of art mirroring life.

Despite everyone being on edge — or maybe because of it — the rehearsal had gone smoothly. Just a few fluffed lines which Kramer had ignored, allowing the play to roll on.

Though she was sure there would be plenty of notes when the last speech was delivered.

Then tomorrow, the grand opening.

She kept glancing to the wings hoping to see that Jack was back, wondering what he found in Kramer's cottage.

But she only saw Todd, hand on the curtain ropes. Jack had told him that he'd be gone, but it seemed to Sarah that he'd been away for far too long.

And Sarah knew the play needed both of them to carry out the finale.

She sensed Ferris shift on his feet, standing next to her.

Everyone edgy, but Ben Ferris — more than anyone — seemed eager for this to be over.

What must it be like for a real writer to perform such creaky stuff as this?

Ferris, as the butler, kept his eyes locked on Goode who took a step towards Kramer.

"You sir — are a *scoundrel*! To think you could come here, woo my sweet Clarissa and abscond with the Pearl of Bombay? You must think me a fool."

Kramer, in character, grinned and turned to the assembled party, making eye contact with each one of them.

Sarah had to admit... he was making this all seem quite real.

"Indeed, sir, the information that you are, indeed, a fool would come as no news to *this* assembled party."

He took a step towards Ellie, who also, acting her socks off, wore a dewy-eyed look of love in her eyes.

Kramer reached out and stroked Ellie's cheek, his fingers lingering as if testing the quality of some fine material.

"Your daughter loves me, and we shall be wed—"

"Over my *dead* body, Collins."

Kramer snapped around on that.

"Oh, I don't think it will be that drastic. True love always finds a way, isn't that right..." back to Ellie, "my sweet?"

"And the Pearl that you have stolen?"

Kramer's hands opened, as if the lack of logic on the part of Lord Blake was transparent.

"I see no evidence of any thievery. Just—"

Kramer turned back to Ambrose Goode: "An old, befuddled man who has misplaced something of tremendous value."

Sarah had to admit: this was fun, the two of them going at

it, "eating the scenery".

And just then she heard — clear, sharp, even here, from deep inside the theatre — the screech of tires.

Jack. Had to be. He was back.

But Sarah kept her eyes on the scene, in character, while her mind raced with thoughts of what Jack may have found …

QUICKLY, JACK HAD pulled his Sprite up to the stage door. Not a parking space, but every second counted.

He popped open the car and then raced to the door, yanking it open, and raced on, into the dark corridors of the backstage.

Past the empty dressing rooms — everyone out on the stage for the big final scene.

Quiet.

So he was in time. But he could guess, only minutes away.

He took a turn at the corner and up the few steps to the backstage area where he could finally hear the lines of the play.

Where Ambrose Goode — Lord Blake — was about to do something to shock the other characters, and hopefully the audience as well.

Without realising how shocking it was actually going to be.

Jack kept racing to the stage. Towards Todd, who heard his steps, turned, put up a finger, indicating that Jack should be quiet.

But Jack didn't cut his pace at all.

Until he heard Tony Standish, in his role as the wealthy American say, "Now, now Lord Blake, I think this has gone *quite* far enough. The lieutenant here is perfectly honourable…"

Jack raced past Todd. He saw Goode pull out the gun and

point it squarely at Jez Kramer's chest.

Were the actors turning and looking at him?

Jack couldn't tell, so he focused on Goode's hand on the gun.

Jack yelled, "Stop! Don't—"

But Goode was lost to the scene and as Jack ploughed into the old man, Goode fired the gun.

The shot — loud, so loud — and Jack didn't know where the round had gone.

The force of Jack's tackle sent Goode flying backwards, on to the set's ornate couch as around him he heard screams of shock and surprise...

But the gun flew out of Goode's hand.

And Jack quickly spun around as soon as he crash-landed on the sofa.

To see; Kramer, staggering backwards, his arm hit, bloody.

But then to the gun, on stage, as Ben Ferris scooped it up, and once again pointed it Kramer who probably wanted to know... *what the hell is going on?*

JACK GOT TO his feet fast.

He saw Sarah turning to the writer, the butler, now centre stage with the gun squarely pointed at Kramer's head.

Jack kept his voice low.

"Ben..."

Kramer lay curled up on the stage floor, right hand locked on his left bicep to stem the blood. His eyes wide with fear.

"I guess I'll have to do this myself," Ferris said quietly.

No one on stage moved.

Not now that everyone knew that the gun fired real bullets.

Sarah stood near Ben — close enough to reach out, maybe

even to wrestle the gun away from him.

I hope she doesn't do that, Jack thought.

Jack had been in situations like this before. Sometimes they could be defused. But often they couldn't, and it became a case of keeping the damage to a minimum.

Jack didn't like Kramer.

But there was no way he could let him be shot again.

Jack took another step closer to Ferris. He also caught Sarah's eyes locked on him. He looked right at her — hoping his eyes told the story.

Don't move.

But Ferris's eyes also shifted towards Jack, then back to Kramer again. He saw the one-time writer's finger tightening on the trigger, and he was still feet away.

"You're a maniac!" Kramer said, his voice shaking.

Not exactly helpful words, Jack thought.

Until he realised that — in a way — they were.

17.

THE REAL VILLAIN

SARAH'S EYES WERE on Jack.

If ever she had to believe that he could use all his skills, it was now.

But at this moment — Kramer wounded, the cast backed up around him, the gun aimed right at Kramer's head — what could Jack do?

Even if he bolted and leaped at Ferris, that left plenty of time for the trigger to be pulled.

But then she saw Jack do something... amazing.

He smiled.

Then — he raised his hands a bit, waist high, palms open.

"Ben. I don't have a weapon. Don't have anything. I just want to tell you something."

Ben Ferris didn't move from his position. But he nodded, then a mumbled "Yes?"

"I went to Kramer's cottage. Saw it trashed."

Another nod.

"I saw his award for *The Fading Light*. And who really wrote it. You're no maniac."

He paused.

"You're a great writer."

"What?" Kramer started to say. A quick glance from Jack stopped Kramer in his tracks.

Sarah saw the slightest movement, as Ferris turned slightly in Jack's direction.

What was going on? she wondered.

Kramer again interrupted the moment: "Isn't anybody going to do *something?*"

Nobody responded to him.

"I saw the award, and — what is it you call it? — the credit for writing. Listed only Jez Kramer."

Jack paused.

"*You* wrote that programme. I've seen it, Ben. It was — really — brilliant."

Now Ferris nodded. "He's a *thief*. Stole the credit, had me booted off the show I created. When he showed up here, in my village… it brought it all back. Doesn't even remember me, my name… right? Just some nameless, faceless writer. So easily disposed of, just as I can—"

Sarah felt her stomach tighten. Each second this went on seemed a second closer to the inevitable happening — Kramer being killed on stage.

"Right. Stolen. Like, well, so many writers, hmm? That person lying on the floor before you is a thief. No wonder you wanted to hurt him."

What is Jack's game here? Sarah thought.

"Who wouldn't?"

"Only what he deserves," Ferris said.

"Right. But you Ben. Is *this* what you deserve? Sure, payback for Kramer. The lowlife who stole your work. But you, the rest of your life in jail? Who wins then, Ben?"

A few seconds of quiet.

Jack took another step, and Sarah saw he kept his hands up

and open.

Must be a NYPD technique.

And she thought: *Jack's done things like this before.*

For the first time, she had a flicker of hope that this might not end in more bloodshed.

"If you kill him, Ben, who wins then? But if you stop now. If you lower that gun, we all know what Kramer did. Everyone in this room. And you can still have a life."

"They'll still send me to jail."

He's actually considering it! Sarah could hardly breathe.

"Sure. For a while. But — least in my country, probably here too — not for the rest of your life." Jack took a breath. "You can have a life. You can even write again. I, for one, would want to see that."

"I don't write anymore."

Jack waited. Then: "You could. But if you pull that trigger, in my book, you lose, and Kramer kind of wins. Don't think anyone on this stage wants that."

Ben didn't move. His arm outstretched, gun at an angle, aiming at Kramer who was probably praying that Jack's words would have some effect.

For a few seconds — nothing.

No talking. No gunshot. The street sounds outside muffled by the thick stone walls of the theatre.

Then:

"Ben. Why not put the gun down?"

As if the idea had just occurred to Jack. Sarah had now trained her eyes on Ben Ferris, as probably everyone else on stage had as well.

Then, as if it had become too heavy, wavering a bit, then so slowly… Ferris lowered the weapon.

Still, no one moved but Jack.

Who now closed the distance between him and the would-be killer.

Jack patted Ben Ferris's shoulder, nodding. Then, he reached down as if removing something unwanted, and slipped the gun out of Ben Ferris's hand.

"Thanks for listening to me, Ben."

Ben finally turned to Jack and nodded back at him.

Then Sarah — and she guessed everyone on else on stage — took a deep breath…

18.

THE PERFORMANCE

THE ACTORS FORMED a line and bowed again, even Graham returning to stand on stage with his replacement, Phil Nailor. Two 'bobbies' on the stage!

Then Todd raised the curtain once more, as the audience kept on clapping.

Sarah turned to her current butler, smiling, hands joined like all the other cast members.

Jack grinned back.

"Guess they liked it?"

Out to the audience, Sarah could see people standing up now, even hear whistles and cheers.

Not so sure that was totally for the performance, Sarah guessed.

After last night's dress rehearsal, Jack had walked Ben over to the police station where — he told her later — Alan was amazed at the story.

Ben cheated by Kramer of credit and the award, leaving the writer too ashamed to ever breathe a word of what had happened. And then using this opportunity for revenge, to stage what would have ultimately been a fatal accident. Setting up the other "mishaps" as cover for his real intentions.

At the station, in front of Alan, Ben didn't deny any of it.

Alan also picked up on Jack's suggestion that they do all they could to help Ben Ferris.

There would be jail time — no doubt. But maybe he could use that time to begin writing again.

"Love to see a novel from you," Jack had said.

Funny.

Could be, Sarah thought, *just as Jack said...*

By not killing Kramer, Ben Ferris might well have got his life back.

But there had been the little problem of the butler being arrested. The entire troupe had convinced Jack to take the role, despite the fact that he'd have to keep the script in his back pocket.

"Guess being a butler serving cocktails won't be too much of a stretch?" Jack had said.

And if Tony Standish's American accent produced laughs, Jack's attempt at a servant's British accent was something to hear.

At many points, *The Purloined Pearl* teetered awfully close to farce.

But the show *worked.* Even the now more-despised Kramer was able to carry on, his wound a mere grazing and, with his arm in a sling, Lieutenant Henry Collins actually seemed a tad dashing.

The curtain came down, everyone beaming at each other.

Most of the audience knew of the events of the past twenty-four hours. Still, it seemed like they'd all had a ball watching the show.

The theatre's future, at least tonight, looked secure.

The curtain went up one more time.

Another big bow from the line of actors.

Which is when Sarah's mum did something unexpected. She broke ranks from the line of players, and strode to the apron.

She put her hands up, signalling silence.

"Ladies and gentlemen, we — the Cherringham Players — want to thank you for your great reception tonight in this, our new home! The restored Cherringham Little Theatre!"

Thunderous applause.

"We hope for many more productions in the years to come. But—"

And now Helen Edwards turned, and looked right at Sarah and Jack.

"...tonight, as you all know, would not have been possible without the invaluable assistance of two people who — whether they decide to continue acting with us or not — will always be part of our little village theatre."

"Did not expect this," Jack said quietly to Sarah.

"She *is* theatrical," Sarah said. "Nothing like a good surprise."

"My own daughter, Sarah, and our village's good friend from America, Detective Jack Brennan!"

"Retired," Jack said, under his breath.

And another wave of applause for just the two of them.

Jack laughed as he looked at Sarah and shook his head.

She heard Tony Standish on his left, whisper.

"Go on you two — take a bow!"

And then with a look to synchronise the move, she and Jack stepped forward and took their bow.

For saving the show, the village theatre and, just maybe, *two* lives.

PLAYING DEAD

NEXT IN THE SERIES:

CHERRINGHAM
A COSY CRIME SERIES

A DEADLY CONFESSION

Matthew Costello & Neil Richards

On the edge of Cherringham lies St. Francis' Convent, home of the Sisters of St. Francis, a small Catholic teaching order. Here a handful of nuns worship, contemplate, and pray. And here one Easter the beloved local priest Father Byrne meets his unexpected demise.

The circumstances of the death are suspicious, and soon Jack and Sarah are on the case: what secrets did Father Byrne take to the grave? Who wanted him dead? And is religious faith ever a guarantee of innocence?

ABOUT THE AUTHORS

Matthew Costello (US-based) and **Neil Richards** (UK) have been writing TV scripts together for more than twenty years. The best-selling Cherringham series is their first collaboration as fiction writers: since its first publication as ebooks and audiobooks the series has sold over a million copies.

Matthew is the author of many successful novels, including *Vacation* (2011), *Home* (2014) and *Beneath Still Waters* (1989), which was adapted by Lionsgate as a major motion picture. He has written for The Disney Channel, BBC, SyFy and has also written dozens of bestselling games including the critically acclaimed *The 7th Guest*, *Doom 3*, *Rage* and *Pirates of the Caribbean*.

Neil has worked as a producer and writer in TV and film, creating scripts for BBC, Disney, and Channel 4, and earning numerous Bafta nominations along the way. He's also written script and story for over 20 video games including *The Da Vinci Code* and *Broken Sword*.